ALSO BY DAVID DIOP

At Night All Blood Is Black

BEYOND
THE
DOOR
OF NO
RETURN

BEYOND
THE
DOOR
OF NO
RETURN

DAVID DIOP

Translated from the French by Sam Taylor

FARRAR, STRAUS AND GIROUX · NEW YORK

Farrar, Straus and Giroux
120 Broadway, New York 10271

Title-page art by Artinblackink / Shutterstock.

Library of Congress Cataloging-in-Publication Data
Names: Diop, David, 1966– author. | Taylor, Sam, 1970– translator.
Title: Beyond the door of no return / David Diop ; translated from
    the French by Sam Taylor.
Other titles: Porte du voyage sans retour.
English Description: First American edition. | New York : Farrar,
    Straus and Giroux, 2023.
Identifiers: LCCN 2023008697 | ISBN 9780374606770 (hardcover)
Subjects: LCSH: Adanson, Michel, 1727–1806—Fiction. |
    LCGFT: Biographical fiction. | Novels.
Classification: LCC PQ3989.2.D563 P6713 2023 | DDC 843/.92—
    dc23/eng/20230501
LC record available at https://lccn.loc.gov/2023008697

Our books may be purchased in bulk for promotional, educational, or
business use. Please contact your local bookseller or the Macmillan
Corporate and Premium Sales Department at 1-800-221-7945, extension
5442, or by email at MacmillanSpecialMarkets@macmillan.com.

www.fsgbooks.com
www.twitter.com/fsgbooks • www.facebook.com/fsgbooks

1   3   5   7   9   10   8   6   4   2

To my wife: I weave these words for you and your silky laughter.

To my beloved children, and to their dreams.

To my parents, messengers of wisdom.

Eurydice—Mais, par ta main ma main n'est plus pressée!

Quoi, tu fuis ces regards que tu chérissais tant!

Eurydice—But my hand by yours is no longer held tight!

Why do you flee my eyes which you once loved so?

—Gluck, *Orpheus and Eurydice*
(Libretto translated from German to French by Pierre-Louis Moline for
the premiere on August 2, 1774, at the Théâtre du Palais-Royal in Paris)

BEYOND
THE
DOOR
OF NO
RETURN

I

Michel Adanson watched himself die under his daughter's gaze. He was wasting away, racked by thirst. His joints were like fossilized shells of bone, calcified and immobile. Twisted like the shoots of vines, they tormented him in silence. He thought he could hear his organs failing one after another. The crackling noise in his head, heralding his end, reminded him of the first faint noises made by the bushfire he'd lit one evening more than fifty years before on a bank of the Senegal River. He'd had to quickly take refuge in a dugout canoe, from where—accompanied by the *laptots*, his guides to the river—he'd watched an entire forest go up in flames.

The sump trees—desert date palms—were split by flames surrounded by yellow, red, and iridescent blue sparks that whirled around them like infernal flies. The African fan palms, crowned by smoldering fire, collapsed in on themselves, shackled to the earth by their massive roots. Beside the river, water-filled mangrove trees boiled before exploding in shreds of whistling flesh. Farther off toward the horizon, the fire hissed as it consumed the sap from acacias, cashew trees, ebony and eucalyptus trees while the creatures of the forest fled, wailing in terror. Muskrats, hares, gazelles, lizards, big cats, snakes of all sizes slid into the river's dark flow, preferring the risk of drowning to the certainty of being burned alive. Their splashes distorted the reflection of the flames in the water. Ripples, little waves, then stillness.

Michel Adanson did not believe he'd heard the forest moan that night. But as he was consumed by an internal conflagration just as violent as the one that had illuminated his dugout on the river, he started to suspect that the burning trees must have screamed curses in a secret plant language, inaudible to men. He would have cried out, but no sound could escape his locked jaw.

The old man brooded. He wasn't afraid of dying, but he regretted that his death would be of no use to science. In a final show of loyalty to his mind, his body, retreating before the great enemy, counted off its successive surrenders almost imperceptibly. Methodical even unto death, Michel Adanson lamented his powerlessness to describe in his notebooks the defeats of this final battle. Had he been able to speak, Aglaé could have acted as his secretary during his final agony. But it was too late to dictate the story of his own death.

He hoped desperately that Aglaé would discover his notebooks. Why hadn't he simply left them to her in his will? He had no reason to fear his daughter's judgment as though she were God. When you pass through the door to the next world, you cannot take your modesty with you.

On one of his last lucid days, he had understood that his research in botany, his herbaria, his collections of shells, his drawings would all disappear in his wake from the surface of the earth. Amid the eternal churn of generations of human beings crashing over one another like waves would come a man, or—why not?—a woman, another botanist who would unceremoniously bury him under the sands of his ancient science. So the essential thing was to figure in the memory of Aglaé as himself and not merely as some immaterial, ghostly scholar. This revelation had struck him on January 26, 1806: precisely six months, seven days, and nine hours before the beginning of his death.

That day, an hour before noon, he'd felt his femur break under the thick flesh of his thigh. A muffled crack, with no apparent cause, and he almost fell headfirst into the fireplace. Had it not been for Mr. and Mrs. Henry, who had caught him by the sleeve of his bathrobe, he might well have ended up with more bruises and perhaps some burns on his face. They laid him out on his bed and went to get help. And while the Henrys ran through the streets of Paris, he tried to press the heel of his left foot hard against the top of his right foot to extend his injured leg and allow the fractured bones in his femur to snap back into place. He fainted from the pain. When he woke, just before the arrival of the surgeon, Aglaé was on his mind.

He did not deserve his daughter's admiration. Until then, his only goal in life had been that his "Universal Orb," his masterpiece, should elevate him to the summit of the botanical world. The pursuit of glory, the jealous recognition of his peers, the respect of scientists all over Europe . . . all of this was mere vanity. He had used up his days and nights meticulously describing close to one hundred thousand "existences"—plants, shellfish, animals of all species—to the detriment of his own. Now, though, he was forced to admit that nothing on earth existed without human intelligence to give it meaning. He would give meaning to his own life by writing it down for Aglaé.

After the unwitting blow dealt to his soul nine months earlier by his friend Claude-François Le Joyand, regrets had begun to torment him. Until then, they had been no more than little sighs of remorse rising up like air bubbles from the bottom of a muddy pond, bursting here and there on the surface without warning, despite the traps his mind had set to contain them. But during his convalescence he had finally managed to master them, to fix them in words. As though divinely ordained, his memories had poured out in order onto the pages of his notebooks, strung together like the beads of a rosary.

Writing had brought him to tears—tears that Mr. and Mrs. Henry attributed to his thighbone. He had let them believe this, let them procure for him all the wine they could get their hands on, replacing the sugar water that he usually drank with a pint and a half of Chablis every day. But drunkenness was not enough to dim the pain of remembering, through the words he wrote in his notebooks, the intensity of his love for a young woman whose features he could barely recall. The contours of her face seemed to have been burned away in the hell of his forgetfulness. How could he translate into simple words the exaltation he had felt when he first saw her fifty years before? In writing about her, he had struggled to restore her to wholeness. And that had been his first battle against death. He had thought it a victory until death caught up with him again. By then, thankfully, he had finished writing his memoirs of Africa. Ripples, little waves of melancholy, and finally resurrection.

Aglaé watched her father die. By the light of a candle placed on his nightstand, a low cabinet with false drawers, he was withering before her eyes. There, in the middle of his deathbed, it seemed to her that only the tiniest fragment of her father remained. He was as thin and dried-up as kindling. In the frenzy of his death throes, his bony limbs gradually lifted up the surface of the sheets that held them down, as if each had its own independent life. Only his enormous head, reclining on a sweat-soaked pillow, emerged from the fabric in which his meager body seemed to be drowning.

This man who had once had long auburn hair, which he would tie in a ponytail with a black velvet ribbon whenever he dressed up to take her out of the convent and drive her to the Jardin du Roi on warm spring days, was now bald. The white down that glistened in the flickering dance of candlelight could not hide the thick blue veins that ran below the surface of the thin skin covering his skull.

Barely visible beneath his bushy gray brows, his blue eyes, sunk deep in their sockets, were glazing over. The fire in those eyes was going out, and, of all the markers of his decline, Aglaé found this the most unbearable. Her father's eyes *were* his life.

He had used them to examine the tiniest details of thousands of plants and animals, to tease out the secrets hidden within their sinuous veins, whether filled with sap or blood.

That power to penetrate the mysteries of life, which his eyes had gained from entire days spent scrutinizing specimens, was still palpable when their gaze was turned on Aglaé. His eyes probed her to her very depths, and her thoughts—even the most secret, the most microscopic of them—were seen. In such moments she was not merely one of God's creations among many others, but became one of the essential links in the great universal chain. Used to scrutinizing the infinitesimal, his eyes suspended her against the boundless background of infinity as if she were a star fallen from the sky, put back in its precise place alongside billions of others, having thought itself lost forever.

Now drawn inward by suffering, her father's gaze no longer had anything to tell her.

Indifferent to the acrid stench of his sweat, Aglaé leaned close to him as she would have done to an unexpectedly wilting flower. He tried to say something. From very close, she watched his lips move, deformed by the passage of a series of stammered syllables. He pursed his lips, then let a sort of wheeze escape from between them. At first she thought he was saying "*Maman*," but in fact it was something like "*Ma Aram*" or "*Maram*." He kept repeating it, over and over, until the end. *Maram*.

III

If there was one man Aglaé hated as much as she could have loved him, it was Claude-François Le Joyand. Three weeks after the death of Michel Adanson, he had published an obituary that was little more than a tissue of lies. How could this man, who claimed to be her father's friend, have written that Adanson's servants, the Henrys, had been the only people at his side during the final six months of his life?

As soon as the Henrys had told her that her father was dying, she had rushed to him from her estate in Bourbonnais. As for Claude-François Le Joyand, she had not seen him appear once during her father's long decline. Nor had she seen him at his funeral. And yet this man had presumed to narrate Michel Adanson's last days as if he himself had witnessed them. At first she wondered if the Henrys had been Le Joyand's malicious informers. But then, remembering their silent tears, the sobs they had stifled so as not to disturb her in her grief, Aglaé had reproached herself for suspecting them of such vileness.

She had read the obituary only once, devouring its several pages, eager to find a graciousness that never appeared, drinking it down to its dregs. No, never could Le Joyand have found her father shivering with cold on a winter evening, crouched in front of the meager fire in his hearth, sitting on the floor and writing by the light of a few embers. No, she had not left her father in such penury that he would have been reduced to consuming nothing but milky coffee. No, Michel Adanson had not been alone when he faced death, as that man pretended: he had been with his daughter.

The purpose of that article, though she could not fathom the reason behind it, seemed to have been to burden her with public shame on top of her grief. It was impossible to refute the insinuations of a supposed friend of her father's. She would probably never have an opportunity to hold him accountable for his spitefulness. Perhaps it was better that way.

Her father's last words on his deathbed had really been "*Ma Aram*" or "*Maram*," and not that ludicrous little cliché that Le Joyand had put in his mouth with his abominable obituary: "Farewell—immortality is not of this world."

As a little girl, Aglaé had been almost perfectly happy on those days, once a month, when her father would drive her in a carriage to the Jardin du Roi. There, he would show her the life of plants. He had counted fifty-eight families of flowers, but, when seen through a microscope, none of them resembled their own family members. His predilection for the oddities of nature, so prone to infringing its own laws beneath an apparent uniformity, had gotten the better of him. Often, early in the morning, the two of them would walk the paths inside the giant greenhouses, pocket watch in hand, marveling at the unvarying hour when the hibiscus flowers, irrespective of their variety, would open their corollas to the light of day. Since then, thanks to him, she had learned the art of bending over a flower for days on end, studying its mysteries.

The intimacy that had blossomed between them at the end of his life made Aglaé regret even more bitterly that she had never truly known Michel Adanson. When she came to visit him, on rue de la Victoire, before his broken femur, before his fall, she had invariably found him squatting, knees touching his chin, fingers in the black earth of a greenhouse he'd had built at the bottom of his small garden. He welcomed her always with the same words, as if trying to transform them into a legend: the reason he squatted like that rather than sit in a chair was that he had gotten used to the position during the five years of his trip to Senegal. She ought to try this resting position, he would tell her, even if it might not appear very elegant. And he would repeat this in the way of very elderly people who cling to their oldest memories, no doubt amused to see flickering in her eyes the same imaginings she had had as a little girl, on the rare occasions when he had told her bits and pieces about his voyage to Africa.

Aglaé was always surprised by the way the images conjured by her father's words seemed to shift shape in her mind. Sometimes she imagined him as a younger man, lying in a cradle of warm sand, surrounded by Africans resting, like him, in the shade of the tall kapok trees. Other times she saw him encircled by the same people in multicolored costumes, taking refuge with them inside the immense trunk of a baobab, sheltering from the African heat.

This flux of imagined memories, summoned by words like "sand," "kapok tree," "Senegal River," and "baobab," had for a moment brought them closer. But for Aglaé, that had not been enough to make up for the time they had wasted avoiding each other—he, because he did not have a minute to spare for his daughter; she, in retaliation for what she had perceived as a lack of love.

When, aged sixteen, she had gone with her mother to stay in England, Michel Adanson had not written her a single letter. He had not had time; like so many others in the age of encyclopedias and philosophes, he had chained himself to his work. But while Diderot and d'Alembert—and, later,

Panckoucke—had each been supported by a hundred or so collaborators, her father had not allowed a single other person to write any of the thousands of articles in his magnum opus. And he had started to forget the time when he still believed it possible to untangle the threads, hidden in the vast skein of the world, which supposedly linked all beings through secret networks of kinship.

The year he got married, he had begun to calculate the head-spinning amount of time it would take to complete his universal encyclopedia. If he assumed, optimistically, that he would die at seventy-five, that gave him thirty-three years. Working an average of fifteen hours a day, that made 180,675 hours of useful time remaining. From that moment on, he had lived as if each minute of attention granted to his wife and his daughter was tearing him away from a labor of love that they were preventing from reaching fruition.

So Aglaé had sought out another father—and found him in Girard de Busson, her mother's lover. If nature had been able to fuse Girard de Busson and Michel Adanson into a single man, this human graft would, in her eyes, have come close to perfection.

No doubt her mother had thought the same thing. It was she, Jeanne Bénard, far younger than Michel Adanson, who had wished to separate from him, despite still being in love. Her husband had willingly acknowledged, before a notary, that it was impossible for him to devote time to his family. Those sincere, if cruel, words had caused Jeanne such pain that she had reported them to her nine-year-old daughter. And when, while still a young girl, Aglaé had discovered that one of her father's books was entitled *Families of Plants*, she had remarked to herself that those plants were in truth his only family.

Where Michel Adanson was short and thin, Antoine Girard de Busson was tall and strong. Where the former could suddenly become taciturn and disagreeable in company, the latter—whom Aglaé called "Monsieur" in the privacy of the mansion to which he welcomed them, she and her mother, after her parents' divorce—was cheerful and sociable.

A connoisseur of the human soul, Girard de Busson had made no attempt to supplant the girl's father in her affections. In fact, he had even continued to help Michel Adanson in his mythical publishing project, ignoring the misanthropic scientist's often rather rude rejections.

Unlike Michel Adanson, who never seemed to care much about Aglaé's eventual marriages or his own grandchildren, Girard de Busson did everything he could to make her happy. He it was who provided her with the dowry she brought to her two unfortunate husbands, and, most significantly of all, it was he who bought for her the Château de Balaine in 1798. But, as though confusing her resentment for her father with her feelings toward him, she sometimes treated him harshly. For his part, Girard de Busson, who had no children of his own, patiently tolerated her abuse, even appearing happy that she should treat him so badly, as if seeing in her fits of rage the evidence of filial love.

Attempting to use her daughter's marriage to expunge the dishonor brought down on her by her divorce, Aglaé's mother had insisted that she marry, at the tender age of seventeen, a conventional military man named Joseph de Lespinasse, who, on their wedding night, unwisely decided to attack her virginity *manu militari*. When the two of them were alone together in their bedchamber, this man dared to do the unforgivable. Assuming she was gripped by the same desire, he whispered to her, in a voice made hoarse by lust, that he wanted to possess her *more ferarum*, like a wild animal. This crude intimation in Church Latin had sickened her less than the brutal way he had attempted to give rein to his passion. In the end, she defended her body at the expense of his. Joseph de Lespinasse, a notorious carouser, had not been able to leave the house for a week afterward due to the purplish bruise that ornamented the periphery of his right eye. Barely a month later, she had obtained a divorce from him without difficulty.

Aglaé had been no more happy with Jean-Baptiste Doumet, a sublieutenant in a cavalry regiment who became a merchant in Sète. Her second husband's only merit was to have given her two sons while strictly respecting the rules of procreativity without passion. If he had any peculiar tastes when it came to the bedroom, he did not practice them on her. Perhaps he reserved them for the women of those one-night stands, which, not long after their wedding, he made no attempt to conceal from her.

She feared she would never be happy. The idea that happiness in love existed only in books saddened her. And, even though she had experienced enough of life to put such sentimental illusions behind her, she could not help hoping, even after two failed marriages, that one day she would find the love of her life at first sight. Her faith in Love made her angry with herself. She was like one of those atheists who fear they will succumb to the temptation to believe in God on the day of their death. She cursed Eros without ever being able to renounce him completely.

So when Girard de Busson, seeing her in this melancholic state, told her he had bought the Château de Balaine and that she could visit it a month later, she felt herself come back to life. Before even seeing it, she decided that the château would be her refuge. People, plants, and animals—all would live there together in harmony. Balaine would be her private masterpiece, a work known only to Aglaé herself. She alone would be able to tabulate, once the project had come to fruition, everything that it had cost her. At Balaine, she would cherish even her disappointments.

V

Located not far from the town of Moulins, in the Marches du Bourbonnais, the Château de Balaine adjoined the small village of Villeneuve-sur-Allier, with its population of just under seven hundred souls. The first time Girard de Busson took her there, it was just the two of them. Jean-Baptiste, her second husband, had been thrilled to find himself alone in Paris and had not wished to accompany her, while Émile, their elder son, was still too young for such a journey and had been left in the care of his grandmother Jeanne.

Ensconced inside Girard de Busson's luxurious carriage, drawn by four horses driven, as always, by Jacques, the family coachman, they left the house at dawn on June 17, 1798. Girard de Busson's mansion was on rue du Faubourg-Saint-Honoré, close to the Folie Beaujon. They crossed the Seine by the Pont de la Concorde, but, after passing through Saint-Germain, Jacques chose to head south and then east, riding alongside the old city wall, from gate to gate. He wished to avoid the popular quarters of Saint-Michel, Saint-Jacques, and, above all, Saint-Marcel, from where they could also have reached the Barrière d'Italie via rue Mouffetard. Girard de Busson's carriage was a clear sign of his wealth. And, this being the era of the Directoire, the working classes, still nostalgic for the glory days of the Revolution, were easily enraged.

Beyond the Barrière d'Italie lay the king's road, renamed in the time of Napoleon the "Imperial Road no. 8," which connected Paris to Lyon. Aglaé had rarely left Paris by the Route du Bourbonnais. Farther on, they stopped in Nemours, where fashionable Parisians liked to spend warm spring Sundays parading in open-top carriages.

Her eyes were half-closed as they began the long journey toward the Château de Balaine, her thoughts turned inward. She sat with her back to the direction of travel—facing Girard de Busson, who silently respected her feigned drowsiness—and paid no attention to the landscape moving slowly past the windows, letting herself be soothed by the gentle swaying. Little by little, in the half light of dawn, she began to imagine that the carriage's creaking springs, mingled with the muffled clop-clop of the horses' hooves, were the creak of the rigging and the whistle of wind in the sails of a ship anchored at the distant edges of the Atlantic. Then, suddenly, the brightness that had filled the interior of the carriage through the eastern window disappeared, as if, reversing the usual passage of time, night had followed dawn. A wave of murky light fell over them, swallowing her in a half sleep conducive to waking dreams. They had just passed the Carrefour de l'Obélisque and were now sinking softly into the Forêt de Fontainebleau.

She was standing on the bridge of a ship winged with white sails. Beneath her feet, the wooden boards radiated heat. Above her stretched a dusk of blue, orange, and green clouds, melting into a vaporous golden sky. Clouds of flying fish pursued by invisible predators splashed the boat's hull. Their fins could not propel them fast enough to escape the danger menacing them under the water's surface. Soaring toward the sky, they fled the wide-open pink mouths that surged upward from the ocean's depths. But they were also being hunted from above by white birds: cormorants or seagulls, perhaps. And those silver-flashing arrows—half fish, half bird—were snatched by sharp beaks and crushed by powerful jaws amid bouquets of foam.

With her eyes still closed, feeling as desperate as those strange fish that were at home neither in water nor in air, she fought back her tears.

Later, this was all that Aglaé would remember of that first journey to the Château de Balaine in June 1798: her sad half-conscious dream, from which she thought she could wake whenever she wished. But the dream had pursued her all the way to their destination. It was only during the many, often solitary journeys that she undertook during the years prior to September 4, 1804—when she moved into a farmhouse near to the Château de Balaine while it was refurbished—that she began to associate her memories with the small towns and villages they passed through between Paris and Villeneuve-sur-Allier.

Montargis in the rain. The black waters of the Canal de Briare. Cosne-Cours-sur-Loire, where she stopped more than once to buy Sancerre wine for her stepfather and her father. Maltaverne, where a surprise storm kept her prisoner in its gloomy inn, the misleadingly named Au Paradis. Chancing to leave La Charité-sur-Loire one morning, she was given the most beautiful view of the river she had ever seen: drowning in mist, the Loire reminded her of the ghostly Thames, which she had looked out on during the year she had spent in London, before her first marriage. In Nevers she bought most of the château's blue and white earthenware crockery. Of the other places she had passed, she recalled nothing.

Girard de Busson had timed their first arrival in Villeneuve-sur-Allier to coincide with the festival of John the Baptist. Just before their entrance into the town, he explained to her that in almost all the villages of Bourbonnais, from dawn on that feast day, they would find—perched on makeshift stages in the middle of markets—peasant men and women hoping to be hired as farmhands or as servants in the houses of the local bourgeoisie. Dressed in their Sunday best, a bouquet of wildflowers tied to their waists, they would sell their labor to the highest bidder for a period of one year. After fierce negotiations over their salary, their new boss would give them a five-franc coin, the "*denier de Dieu*," in exchange for their bouquet. Any peasant not wearing flowers was no longer for sale. Around noon, while the market gardeners and the farmers folded up their stalls following the end of this strange trade in flowers and labor, there would be a huge commotion as the local young people danced wildly in the streets. It was at this point that Aglaé and Girard de Busson's carriage arrived in the village square.

Like gods appearing suddenly from the heavens, they had been the recipients of most of the bouquets that had changed hands that morning, and which a few laughing villagers threw onto the roof of their carriage. And so, pursued for a while by a small band of happy locals, and sowing wildflowers in their wake as the carriage shook its way down the winding path, they discovered the Château de Balaine at the end of a drive-way lined with mulberry trees.

Aglaé did not immediately rush into the arms of her new home. She was content to observe it all, detached enough to collect impressions of the château that she would later associate with positive or negative feelings. She did not fully enter into the experience of her first encounter with Balaine, because she wanted to be able to relive it more easily later, alone with herself. The château had corner turrets on each side of a courtyard in the shape of a capital U: once wide-open to visitors, it was now overgrown with weeds. The windows of the turrets were surrounded by red and white stones, although their colors were now indistinguishable, covered with a tangle of ivy and moss. The façade was rendered ugly by an oversized passageway that ran from one side to the other.

Girard de Busson reeled off the names of some of Balaine's owners since the fourteenth century. The first ones, the Pierreponts, had built it as a fortified castle, then passed it down from generation to generation for almost four hundred years. After 1700, when the Pierrepont lineage ended, there had been a succession of owners until a certain knight from Chabre, who had undertaken a complete reconstruction of the château in 1783 under the direction of Évezard, an architect from Moulins. Intimidated by the sheer scale of the work, the knight had changed his mind and sold it again.

Girard de Busson tried in vain to open the château's front door. A smell of damp plaster and rotting wood escaped through a small crack. They did not manage to get into the entrance hall, but the shutters of the large windows at the back of the building had come loose and they could see beams of sunlight staining the blackish wooden floorboards, covered with a thick layer of dust.

"I've rented a farm close by where you could stay to oversee the renovation work," her stepfather told her, nodding. "We'll spend the night there tonight. But let's walk around the house first."

When they turned around, the few villagers who had followed them there had disappeared. Jacques was busy decorating the horses' harnesses with the bouquets of flowers that had not fallen from the roof while they were driving. To the left of the building, Aglaé and her stepfather walked around a muddy pond, presumably replenished by a small stream nearby. The back of the building was even more overgrown and dilapidated than the façade.

It was then, in that moment, that she was finally aware of a feeling of deep joy rising within her. Thanks to a gift for optimism inherited from her mother, she was able to see beyond the apparent ugliness of an object, or a place, to its potential for beauty. If the faintest hint of vanished splendor had been visible at the back of the building, calling out to her to resurrect its long-lost luster, Aglaé would have ignored it. What she wanted was to be a pioneer, to remake the château according to her own idea of beauty rather than re-create past glories. She could easily imagine the last, debt-ridden Pierrepont, a hundred years earlier, petrified into inaction by the idea of committing the sacrilege of adding even the smallest of modern touches to this old château. Never would she put her descendants in the position of that last Pierrepont, a slave to stone ruins.

No, she would bequeath to her children a place whose living center would be not the château but its grounds, the beauty and rarity of its plants, its flowers, and all the trees that she would plant there. When buildings collapse after four centuries because the men who built them and their descendants' descendants have all died out, it is the trees they planted that survive the onslaught of time. Nature never goes out of fashion, she thought with a smile.

Girard de Busson was secretly watching her, and he rejoiced at the sight of that smile. It was a new way of thanking him, more convincing perhaps than the words of gratitude she had repeated to him but which failed to fully describe for him the fullness of her joy and appreciation.

All the way back to Paris, she told Girard de Busson about her vision for the château's grounds. At the time, they were restricted to a thin strip of land that would have to be enlarged through the purchase of neighboring properties. She would plant American sequoias there, maple trees, southern magnolias. She would construct a greenhouse to cultivate exotic flowers, shoeblack plants with their five large petals. Her father, Michel Adanson, would use his botanical connections to help her bring plants there from all over the world. And Girard de Busson said yes to all of this, in spite of the expense.

That evening, enthused by her first visit to Balaine, Aglaé deluded herself into believing she could interest Jean-Baptiste in her dream by giving herself to him. She wished she could find the words to evoke the eternal happiness that awaited them there, which would win him over as if by magic. But what she ended up saying to him left her disgusted with herself:

"You know where it comes from, the name Balaine? . . . You can't guess? . . . Well, it's because the people of the village have always gone there, to the land around the château, to collect bulrushes to make brooms—*balais*."

"Hence the château's pretty name!" Jean-Baptiste instantly replied. "At least it should be clean then . . . with two crossed brooms for a coat of arms!"

Aglaé was mortified less by Jean-Baptiste's mockery than by the burst of naïve confidence that had led her to forget that her husband was not her friend. But, as if a part of her absolutely had to enter into communion with someone, as if the upheaval in her life was simply bound to touch the person who shared that life, she gave herself to him anyway. Powerless to stop herself seeking out his complicity, she was forced to watch, as if from outside her own body, as she deployed all her charms to mimic a tenderness she never would have believed herself capable of with him.

So, it was probably that very night, after visiting the Château de Balaine for the first time, that she conceived her second son, Anacharsis—and, in the same instant, her plan to divorce Jean-Baptiste Doumet.

VI

There had not been a day, since her first encounter with the Château de Balaine, when she did not dream about her property as if it were a lover. In a sketchbook she traced driveways, detailed flower beds, and designed forests in thick pencil strokes. She told her father about her plans, and Michel Adanson wrote to inform her that he was going to give up his research work for a half day every week so that she could visit him. And so she went to his house on rue de la Victoire almost every Friday, for a "postprandial get-together," as he wrote to her on the invitation in his somewhat old-fashioned French.

Michel Adanson was not the man his fellow Académie members described after his death. It was the great and self-important Lamarck who fostered her father's reputation as a truculent misanthrope. Aglaé imagined that men like her father, who placed honesty and justice above all other considerations and were incapable of compromising their principles even for the sake of their friends, were not well liked. Charm and politeness were not Michel Adanson's strong points: he simply liked someone or he didn't; there was no middle ground. He rarely tried to hide the disgust he felt in the presence of a colleague he did not respect. But over time, and thanks to the wisdom gleaned from Montaigne, whom he advised his daughter to read as well, he learned not to brood for weeks on end whenever someone uttered a word against him.

Her father had welcomed into his greenhouse three green frogs, which he would observe from the corner of his eye while repotting exotic trees for his daughter and the park she was creating at the Château de Balaine. The three of them were almost tame: they would let him approach without fear, and he even called them his "civilized gentlemen." Aglaé did not understand this odd expression until she heard her father address one of those three amphibians with the words: "Monsieur Guettard, behave yourself!" Guettard had been one of Michel Adanson's worst enemies during his final years at the Royal Academy of Sciences in Paris. Seeing her smile, he said with a sparkle of mischief in his eyes that she had never noticed before: "That one isn't venomous like his cousins from the Amazon in French Guiana, but I can assure you that the man whose name he bears did everything he possibly could to poison my life."

Aglaé laughed heartily at this joke, and her father added that the names of Lamarck and de Condorcet, appended to the other two frogs, served to remind him of the role his two colleagues had played in the settlement of his dispute with Guettard. "These days I have trouble telling the three of them apart," he concluded.

At the end of his life her father seemed to turn away from that hunt for the glory that had invariably fled at his approach like a deer sniffing the wind and scenting the presence of a predator. During her last visits to rue de la Victoire, he very rarely mentioned his interminable "Universal Encyclopedia of Natural History." And he became so available, so disposed to really listen to her, that Aglaé at last felt confident enough, one Friday in autumn, in the greenhouse where they both stood, to tell him a secret.

She revealed to him the anguish she had felt, in his company, when she was still a little girl, seeing the astronomical immensity of the universe for the first time. Perhaps he remembered? He had taken her, one summer evening, to an observatory in Saint-Maur, on the outskirts of Paris. Through the telescope, her eye had led her into the void, and, since the light from the stars appeared so cold to her, the idea crossed her mind—shockingly to a little girl who believed unthinkingly in God—that heaven could not be located in the sky. Since earth was merely one minuscule dot in the vastness of infinite space, if God had wanted to provide His children with a heaven and a hell, why would he put them anywhere other than in the place where they already were?

"You imagined God's plans in proportion with your own worries," her father replied. "Perhaps you place heaven in the visible world because you consider it impossible to be happy anywhere other than in your own home. For myself, I believe that heaven and hell exist inside each of us."

Hearing those murmured words, she thought she could see in her father's eyes a sort of hesitation, the sudden appearance of an image, his mind pausing on the recollection of a distant memory. This time, however, his attention did not seem to have fled in the direction of his usual obsessions. It was, she suspected, a project of another nature that he had conceived in that moment, animated by the energy of a spontaneous resolution. Aglaé loved that moment: it was instantly en-graved in her memory even though she could make no sense of it. While he continued to stir up the soil in preparation for her plants, surrounded by his three "civilized gentlemen," and still squatting on the ground like the Senegalese, he appeared to turn his scrutiny upon himself, as if through the lens of a telescope.

VII

Sagging under the weight of the huge parcels tied to its luggage rack, Girard de Busson's luxurious carriage entered the courtyard very slowly. Over a distance of almost three hundred kilometers from Paris, Jacques's four horses had dragged the plethora of crates containing seashells, dried plants, stuffed animals, and even books bequeathed to Aglaé by her father. She would never have believed that Michel Adanson would leave her such a chaotic collection of objects. She would have expected him to sift through and organize them.

She was standing on the doorstep with Pierre-Hubert Descotils, who had come to show her his plans for renovating the château. The young man had looked as surprised as she had at the sight of such a beautiful carriage transformed into a vulgar wagon for freight. Following Évezard, the architect from Moulins who had directed the first reconstruction work on the château twenty years earlier, she had hired Pierre-Hubert Descotils to finish the job. A tall, dark-haired man of haughty bearing with a wide forehead, handsome teeth, and clear eyes, he was a little over thirty years old. The timbre of his voice was remarkable: slightly deep, but not excessively so. He pronounced all his words very precisely but without affectation, lingering upon them a little like a man attempting to conceal a stammer, whose affliction is sometimes betrayed by his efforts to sound natural. This idiosyncrasy intrigued Aglaé throughout the time that they spent together that afternoon.

Her head leaning so close to his, above the plans for the château, that she could hear him quite easily even when he spoke in a whisper, she thought she could detect a hint of shyness in the little inflections of his voice. But she was probably wrong about that because, at the sight of Jacques perched on his carriage among what appeared to be a towering rubbish heap, Pierre-Hubert Descotils burst out laughing—a clear, loud, sonorous laugh that infected Aglaé too. Composing himself again, the architect took his leave of her, smiling thinly as he promised to return once the plans for the château had been corrected in accordance with her "directives."

Vexed by this incident after such a long and exhausting journey, Jacques began to sulk, reacting with stubbornly cold silence to the warm words of welcome Aglaé uttered in an attempt to mollify him. She would never know all the taunts and jeers he had suffered in Paris. Rue Mouffetard in particular had, for him, been hell. A teeming gang of children had escorted him all the way to the Barrière d'Italie, laughing and throwing stones at him while watched by their unreprimanding parents. For the children on that endless-seeming street, his carriage had been a carnival float.

Having moved closer, Aglaé understood why Jacques had been in a bad mood ever since Paris. It wasn't only the roof of the carriage that was cluttered with bundles; the interior too was filled with a jumble of potted plants, books, and various small pieces of furniture in many different shapes. The weight of this bedlam of objects was enormous. Aglaé knew that Jacques loved his four horses as if they were friends and must have found it hard to watch them sweating as they climbed the long slopes up to La Charité-sur-Loire. So she apologized solemnly and sincerely for having laughed when he entered the courtyard. But Jacques did not forgive her until she ordered Germain, her gardener, to help him to unharness, feed, and water the horses.

When she found herself alone, standing in the middle of the courtyard, she looked up at the sky, where bouquets of lacy turquoise clouds were blossoming in the dusk. Shadows of swifts flitted here and there above her, and their high-pitched cries sent a thrill through her heart. A smell of warm earth enveloped the young woman like a blanket of joy. Aglaé felt her throat tighten with a sweet, deep-seated happiness. She thought she could guess at the cause, but she did not allow herself to put it into words. It was still too early. She would wait until later to analyze her exaltation, to gain a better understanding of it. She promised herself she would bring it out into the clear light of consciousness as soon as everything at the farm was in order.

She knew she felt something, a sort of tenderness, for Pierre-Hubert Descotils. She did not yet dare think that it might be love.

VIII

Michel Adanson threw nothing away. From a chipped terra-cotta pot that had long been in his possession, he one day took some small fragments that he used to drain the soil at the base of a young sapling, then crushed afterward to enrich the soil with mineral dust.

He treated books this way too. He often said that only ten out of a hundred books on botany were worth reading. "And not only that," he added, "but if you excluded all the pages devoted to their authors' academic concessions, to their vanity poorly concealed under a veil of false modesty, you would be left with only five of any use." For him, encyclopedias and dictionaries were the most valuable books because their authors, constrained by the brevity of the form, did not have space to waste on flatteries. Aglaé was not unaware that her father was essentially advocating for his own encyclopedia, the colossal drafts of which would remain forever unfinished. But the weakness for fame that he shared with his colleagues did not lead him—at least in the eyes of his daughter, who ended up deifying him—to confine himself to small objectives. Michel Adanson's ambition at least had the merit of being gargantuan.

As she emptied the carriage of dozens of objects and mismatched pieces of furniture, Aglaé understood, more quickly than she could have imagined, just how subjective the notion of usefulness could be. The heir to a marine spyglass with a broken lens could not work out why her father had been so determined to bequeath it to her. She rummaged through all the drawers of her memory in search of its meaning. Had he left her this collection of incongruous objects precisely so that she would attempt to solve the mystery they posed? Perhaps this was his roundabout way of appearing in her thoughts occasionally after his death. What could be the purpose of this verdigris metal compass, this blunt knife, this rusty oil lamp? What was she to make of this little necklace of white and blue glass beads, or of the scrap of cloth—a fragment of indienne decorated with purple crabs and yellow fish—that she had discovered in the drawer of one of the low cabinets? In the same cabinet she had also found a louis d'or. She couldn't fathom how her thrifty father could have abandoned it there.

Surprised by his strange final wish to encumber her with objects of no apparent value other than that of having once belonged to him, Aglaé nevertheless decided not to throw any of them away, for fear that one day she would regret being separated from an inheritance whose meaning could have been restored to her only through the involuntary work of memory, via the detour of a dream. And she congratulated herself on having made that decision when she exhumed from under one of the carriage's seats a wine crate in which there were three large jars that one might have imagined containing jam, carefully protected by several layers of newspaper, tied up in string.

She cautiously untied the knots, curious to discover what

could be hidden beneath so much paper. It turned out to be Messieurs Guettard, Lamarck, and de Condorcet, her father's three "civilized gentlemen." Finding them preserved in yellowish formalin, with no explanatory labels attached, Aglaé smiled, realizing that through this trio of dead frogs he was bequeathing her a shared, private memory, something known only to the two of them. What had brought them closer in the final years of his life, when she would visit him in his greenhouse almost every Friday afternoon, was right there, at the bottom of those jars. She took this as a warning not to jettison anything until she had clarified the meaning of all these disparate objects. It was like a game whose rules she was expected to work out for herself over the course of time.

Following her father's example, Aglaé had had a greenhouse built in the yard of the farm where she was staying during the renovations to the château. That greenhouse was useful not only for preparing next year's plantings for the château's grounds, which had already been blessed with a certain beauty since she had begun cultivating them in her own way. It was also a place where she could maintain a relationship with her father from beyond the grave, a space where their shared preoccupations could germinate. In this hot, humid setting, saturated with the scent of earth and flowers, Aglaé communed with the late Michel Adanson. Silent solidarities bloomed in the Balaine greenhouse, an infinite reservoir of shared conversations and thoughts. As she gradually acquired the same gardening skills as her father, she conversed with him without words, swapped tips on flowerings and cuttings, inspired by all the things he might have told her had he still been of this world.

IX

Two days after her father's entire legacy had been transferred from the carriage to the greenhouse, she went there very early in the morning. Its glass roof, covered in dewdrops, was starting to steam in the first rays of sunlight. The sky was still quite dark; the air, cool. She could discern the outlines of things, but not the details of their composition or color. It was a small temple of ghostly objects. In their three glass tombs, lined up on a shelf, the "civilized gentlemen" were little more than shapeless masses, drowned in the surrounding dimness.

On top of that same shelf, the shadow of a stuffed owl was raising its wings. And, through an optical illusion that would last until sunlight poured into the greenhouse, Aglaé imagined that this bird was about to swoop down upon her head.

Her plants seemed to have disappeared, swallowed up by the overwhelming disorder of buckets, pitchers, tools of all kinds, and empty pots.

She swore she would tidy up everything that had been hastily pushed against the glass walls by Jacques and Germain. The light could not enter the greenhouse the way it would need to for her grafts to take, her cuttings to bud, and her exotic flowers to survive the coming winter.

Closing the door behind her, Aglaé squatted in the center of the greenhouse as she had seen her father do, in the style of the Senegalese. Daylight slowly crept in, erasing the mystery it had bestowed upon the things around her. Close by, to her left, an inlaid mahogany cabinet about fifty centimeters tall, like a sort of miniature secretaire, displayed its four drawers shining in the morning sunlight. Their handles were four small hands in pale bronze, each folded into a fist except for the index finger. The tabletop was covered with a thick puddle of white wax. Aglaé remembered that it had been on this low nightstand that the last candles had burned, illuminating her father's deathbed.

Just then, in a play of light and shade, she thought she glimpsed, dug into the wooden front of one of those drawers, just below the handle, a sort of three-dimensional design. She leaned down to get a better view. As if indicated by the outstretched bronze index finger, she recognized a flower. No doubt engraved with an awl into the rosewood façade was a hibiscus flower, almost closed in on itself, with a long pistil emerging, crowned with a few bits of pollen in the shape of grains of rice.

She opened the hibiscus drawer and found there the same necklace of white and blue glass beads, the scrap of indienne and the louis d'or that she had already discovered a few days before. After pulling open the three other drawers, however, she noticed that the one with the flower seemed shallower than the others. She tried to pull it out completely, but couldn't. Then, inspired by a sudden, almost involuntary intuition, she pressed down on the exact spot in the drawer's façade marked by the hibiscus engraving. She thought she could feel something click under her index finger, as if a secret mechanism had been triggered by a subtle interplay of tiny springs. And just at that moment, the entire façade of the drawer slid down, revealing, at about one-third of its height, a little shelf, and visible upon it the rounded back of a large dark-red Morocco-leather portfolio. The drawer's false bottom had been so tightly sealed that the leather was completely free of dust.

Giving up her squatting position, Aglaé sat on the floor of the greenhouse. She did not dare open the red portfolio. She felt as uncertain as the hibiscus flower engraved on the façade of the secret drawer: Did it close at nightfall or open at dawn? Aglaé slowly untied the black ribbon that was looped around the portfolio and, on the first page of a large-sheet notebook, found a dried flower. From the fine bright orange filaments embedded in the watermark of the thick paper, she guessed that the flower, when alive, must have been scarlet. A constellation of yellow saffron dots above it: the remains of some pollen, detached from the pistil. On the next page, with almost no margins, Aglaé recognized her father's smooth, elegant, closely spaced handwriting.

Were these notebooks intended for her? It seemed to Aglaé that she had not found them by chance, and that they had been waiting for her these past several months in that false-bottomed drawer. But why had her father taken the risk of their going undiscovered? Why put so many obstacles in the way of her reading them? If she had not wanted to accept all these belongings bequeathed to her, the red leather portfolio would have been lost to her. Perhaps the discovery of these handwritten pages was, for her, the discovery of a hidden, private Michel Adanson, a man she would otherwise never have known.

Aglaé hesitated. She wasn't certain she wanted to know. The first words she read disarmed her.

X

For Aglaé, my beloved daughter,
July 8, 1806

I have collapsed in on myself like a tree devoured from within
by termites. I am speaking not only of the physical collapse,
which you have witnessed in these last months of my life.
Long before my femur snapped, something else broke inside
me. I know precisely when it happened: you will discover
the exact circumstances if you agree to read my notebooks.
When all the screens I erected around my most painful
memories fell to the ground, I realized that I had to tell you
what really happened to me in Senegal. I was only twenty-
three years old when I went there. My story is not the one you
were able to read in my published account of the voyage: it
is, rather, the story of my youth, my first regrets and my last
hopes. I always wished my father had told me about his life,
without shame or modesty, the way I am going to tell you
about mine.

I owe you the truth if I am to have any hope that you will
grant my final wishes. I am not sure how well I have judged
all their practical consequences. It is up to you, my dear

Aglaé, to give them substance, to reinvent them when you are facing the person I will ask you to go and meet for me. Everything, I suspect, will depend upon your reading of my notebooks . . .

I will spare you the burden of publishing my "Universal Orb." You would lose yourself in the labyrinth of my drafts. The Ariadne's thread that I thought I might find, one that would help me to survey all of nature without getting lost, does not exist. I have left the task of publishing extracts of my work to your mother, convinced as I am that this project will fail. Jeanne will not suffer: she knows as well as I do that the publication of my books was always a lost cause. I am a branch cut off from the tree of botany. Linnaeus has won. He will pass into posterity; I will not. I feel no bitterness at that fact. In the end I understood, as I think you realized during the time you spent with me recently, that my thirst for renown, my academic ambitions, my longed-for encyclopedia were mere delusions, created by my mind to preserve me from a terrible suffering that began during my voyage to Senegal. I buried that suffering when I returned to France, long before your birth, but it wasn't dead. Far from it, in fact.

I do not wish to burden you with part of my own guilty feelings, but to let you know what sort of man I am. What more useful legacy can a parent pass on to his children? In any case, this is the only one that seems of any value to me. As I write these lines, I confess my fear of stripping myself naked before you. Not that I fear you would mock me, as Ham did his father, Noah, when he found him asleep on the ground after a night of drinking, his nudity on display before the eyes of his children. I fear only that, as a woman of your time, a prisoner of the vagaries of life, as insensible to others as I could be during part of my existence, you will never find my secret notebooks. I fear your indifference.

To read these pages, you will first have had to agree to keep the legacy of my meager belongings for the sole reason that they were once mine. If you are reading this, it is because you searched for my hidden life and you found it, because you cared about me a little. To love is also to share the memory of a common history. I sought out moments in which our relationship might bloom far too seldom when you were a child, and then when you were an adolescent. I offer my legacy to you now that you have become a woman, now that death has shielded me from your sight and your judgment. I was too busy fleeing myself to devote time to you, and I regret that now. But perhaps the rarity of our shared memories will make them more valuable . . . Small consolation.

If you are reading this, it is because I was not mistaken in believing that you attached importance to our regular outings to the Jardin du Roi when you were still a little girl. I remembered your wonder at the ability of the hibiscus flower, irrespective of its variety—and God knows there are many of them—to alternately open and close with the coming of night and day. Perhaps you remember how you asked me if it was the flower's way of closing its eyes, as we do, at night. "No," I replied, not wanting you to lose your poetic worldview, "it has no eyelids: it sleeps with its eyes open." Do you recall the nickname you gave the hibiscus that day, a name that stuck for some time after? "The flower without eyelids."

So you will not be surprised that I chose the hibiscus as our secret sign. I engraved it on the façade of my little nightstand to show you where the opening mechanism for the false-bottomed drawer was located. The flower without eyelids led you to my notebooks. The hibiscus is the key to my secret, and, if you have found it, it is because I did enough to make you love those few hours we spent together contemplating that wonder of nature.

I hope with all my soul that you will one day read these lines, which mark the beginning of the nameless account of my voyage. I will leave it to you to find it a title. Be a merciful reader. I wish that you might find in my story something to lighten the useless weight commonly attached to life by most men and women, as if life weren't oppressive enough already: the weight of prejudice.

Michel Adanson

Aglaé raised her eyes from the red portfolio. The greenhouse was now bathed in daylight: her father's three "civilized gentlemen" were hideously visible in their jars of formalin, lined up on the shelf facing her. She felt hot, and her legs were stiff. It must surely be close to nine o'clock, and she had much to do before Pierre-Hubert Descotils, the young architect, came that afternoon to submit his revised plans for the château. He had sent her a letter announcing his visit.

Nor did she wish Violette, the cook, or Germain, the gardener—whose services she had hired at the previous festival of John the Baptist—to find her there in the greenhouse, sitting on the floor, her chin quivering like that of a little girl on the verge of tears.

XI

That night, she asked Germain to put the little hibiscus nightstand next to her bed, and on top of it she placed an oil lamp with a shade of etched glass. Sitting up in bed, her back supported by two cushions embroidered with her mother's initials, her legs covered with a heavy gold-colored eiderdown, Aglaé began to read Michel Adanson's notebooks. The flickering of a small flame, its pale yellow light dancing on the pages that she slowly turned, reminded her of the candlelight that had illuminated her father's last moments.

◈

I left Paris for the island of Saint-Louis in Senegal at the age of twenty-three. While others sought to make a name for themselves in poetry, finance, and politics, I wanted to do the same in the science of botany. But, for a reason I did not suspect despite its obviousness, things did not go the way I planned. I made that voyage to Senegal to discover plants, and instead I encountered people.

We are each the fruit of our education, and, like all those who described to me the order of the world, I genuinely believed that what I had been told about the savagery of Black people was true. Why would I have questioned the word of teachers I respected, themselves the heirs of teachers who had assured them that Africans were ignorant and cruel?

The Catholic religion, of which I almost became a servant, teaches that it is natural for Black people to be slaves. I know perfectly well, however, that they are slaves not by some divine decree but because it is convenient to think that way so that we can go on selling them without qualms.

So, I left for Senegal in search of plants, flowers, shells, and trees that no other European scientist had yet described, and what I encountered there was suffering. The inhabitants of Senegal are no less unknown to us than the nature that surrounds them. And yet we believe we know them well enough to claim that they are our natural inferiors. Is this because they appeared poor to us the first time we encountered them, almost three centuries before this? Is it because, unlike us, they did not think it necessary to construct stone palaces strong enough to withstand the erosion that accompanies each passing generation? Can we judge them inferior because they have not built ships that can cross the Atlantic? It is possible that these reasons explain why we do not consider them our equals, but each and every one of them is false.

We always bring the unknown into the realm of the known. Perhaps they did not build stone palaces because they did not think it a useful thing to do. Did we ever stop to wonder if they had other ways of demonstrating the magnificence of their former kings? The palaces, castles, and cathedrals with which we glorify ourselves in Europe are the tribute paid to the rich by hundreds of generations of poor people whose meager hovels no one ever bothered to preserve.

The historical monuments of the Senegalese can be found in their stories, their aphorisms, their tales transmitted from one generation to the next by the griots. The griots' words, which can be as finely wrought as our most beautiful palaces, are their monuments to their kings.

Likewise, the fact that Black people did not build ships to sail to Europe so they could steal our land and enslave us seems to me proof not of their inferiority, but of their wisdom. How can anyone boast about having designed those ships that transport millions of kidnapped innocents to the Americas in the name of our insatiable desire for sugar? Africans do not regard greed as a virtue, as we do unthinkingly, so natural do our own actions appear to us. Nor do they think, as Descartes advised us to do, that we should make ourselves masters and possessors of all nature.

I became aware of our different visions of the world, without finding any reason therein to despise them. Had any European explorer wished to take the trouble to actually know the Africans, he would simply have done what I did: learned one of their languages. And as soon as I knew enough Wolof to understand them without hesitation, I felt as if I were gradually discovering a beautiful landscape that had been heretofore hidden behind a crude reproduction created by a mediocre set designer.

The Wolof language, spoken by the people of Senegal, is every bit the equal of our own. All the treasures of their humanity are compressed within it: their belief in hospitality and fraternity, their poetry, their history, their knowledge of plants, their proverbs, their philosophy of the world. Their language is the key that enabled me to understand that Africans cultivated other riches than those that we pursue aboard our ships. These riches are immaterial. But, in writing this, I do not mean to say that the people of Senegal are somehow separate from the rest of mankind. They are no less human than we are. And, like all humans, their hearts and their minds can thirst for glory and wealth. In Senegal too there are greedy men eager to enrich themselves at the expense of others, to pillage, to massacre for gold. I am thinking of their kings who, like all of ours—up to and including our emperor Napoleon—do not hesitate to enslave people to increase or maintain their power.

My first language instructor was named Madièye. He was a man in his early forties who had worked as an interpreter for several directors general of the Senegal Concession. Madièye, who spoke everyday French quite well, could not translate botanical terms for me. Indeed, only a few initiates—some of them men, others women—knew the medicinal properties of the plants I hoped to study. So I quickly took my leave of Madièye and put my trust in Ndiak, who was just twelve years old when I first met him, and whom I educated in the basics of botany so that he would be of greater help to me when I spoke Wolof to question people with knowledge of that science.

Estoupan de la Brüe, director of the Senegal Concession, had chosen Ndiak for me from the court of the king of Waalo, with whom he had dealings. Ndiak was my guide to Senegal. In his company, and also that of a few armed men supplied by the same king, nothing bad could happen to me. Ndiak told me he was a prince, but that he would never become king of Waalo. It was due to his low ranking in the order of succession to the throne of Waalo that his father had agreed to let Ndiak leave his court, located in Nder, to join me at M. de la Brüe's request. Only the king's nephews on the maternal side could become kings in Senegal. This was what Ndiak explained to me, at our first meeting, in his own inimitable way: "When a child is born to a queen, there is only one certainty: that his veins are filled with blood that is at least half-royal. You can always see the mother's markings on a baby panther, rarely those of the father."

As always when he was joking, Ndiak did not smile as he said this; he could hide his face behind a mask of impassivity despite his desperate urge to burst out laughing. He was betrayed only by his eyelids, which blinked when he was being funny, and perhaps also a certain tension at the corners of his mouth. Ndiak was a great inventor of proverbs, and everyone who knew him could not help loving him.

Ndiak kept telling me that he resembled his mother more than his father. She was the noblest and most beautiful woman in the kingdom of Waalo, possibly in the whole world, and—since he had inherited her beauty—he was quite naturally the most beautiful young man I had ever seen. His features were stunningly regular and symmetrical, as if nature had calculated the proportions of his face using the same golden number as the sculptor of the Apollo Belvedere. I merely nodded and smiled when Ndiak boasted, which encouraged him to say, without laughing, to anyone who would listen: "You see, even this *toubab* Adanson who has seen more lands than all of us put together, including five generations of your ancestors, you who are looking at me with your wide Black eyes . . . even Adanson recognizes that I am the most beautiful of all."

I tolerated his arrogance because I realized that he was using it to overcome the reluctance to speak to me felt by many of the country's experts in botany. They were suspicious of all white men, and of me in particular, since I was asking questions on unusual subjects. Ndiak had a prodigious memory and was a skilled helper when it came to these interviews. Thanks to him I was able to learn a great number of customs that the clerks of the Senegal Concession, including its director, Estoupan de la Brüe, would certainly have benefited from knowing had they wanted to increase the profits of their commerce with the different kingdoms of Senegal.

XII

I first heard about the revenant a little more than two years after my arrival in Senegal.

It happened one night while I was in the village of Sor, located about an hour's walk from the island of Saint-Louis. Ndiak and I had left the fort at daybreak with the intention of collecting plants before traveling to that village, which was extremely difficult to reach from the river. Protected by thorny creepers, barely visible behind its barricade of undergrowth, the path leading to Sor seemed to me unworthy of its proximity to the island of Saint-Louis, where, at the time of my visit to Senegal, more than three thousand people—Black, white, and mixed race—lived around the fort belonging to the director general of the Concession. The lack of care given to maintaining a path that could have massively increased trade and profits between the island of Saint-Louis and the village of Sor seemed, to me, proof of the Africans' negligence. But that very evening, I learned just how wrong I was.

Baba Seck, the chief of the village, to whom I had on several occasions made remarks about the inconvenience of the path leading to Sor, had always been content to reply with a smile that, if it pleased God, the day when Sor would become easier to reach would soon arrive. Even though I found his response lacking, I did not insist because I had warm feelings for Baba Seck, who had, several times, demonstrated to me his wisdom and open-mindedness. He was a tall, affable, and very fat man, about fifty years old, whose natural authority in the eyes of the villagers, his subjects, was heightened by his eloquence.

It was his words that saved me during one of my first visits to the village, when I had killed a sacred serpent in the middle of a village assembly—a viper that was moving dangerously close to my right thigh as I sat there cross-legged on a mat of woven bulrushes. With a single phrase, Baba Seck brought a halt to the wooden staff that his eldest son, Galaye Seck, was about to bring down on my head. With a second phrase, he silenced the roar of the audience as he picked up the serpent's corpse and nimbly slipped it into one of the deep pockets of his tunic. So I accepted his evasive answer, until the night when I realized that the story of the revenant which he told us was a response to my criticisms.

In almost all the Senegalese villages that I visited, there are broad, square stages, about three feet above the ground, supported at their four corners by thick, solid acacia branches. These stages can hold about ten people at most, sitting or lying, and they are made of latticed branches covered with several layers of woven rush mat. They are open-air refuges, not from mosquitoes, of which there are always too many, but from the torrid heat that builds inside the huts during the warmest nights of the year: from June until October. It is there, beneath the starry vault—whose constellations the

Africans know just as well as we do—that they go to breathe fresh air and talk away half the night, ignoring the mosquito bites, before finally falling asleep. Taking turns to tell short tales or brief jokes, or to test their skills in long verbal jousts, the villagers will also sometimes recount darker stories. And it was one of those stories that silenced the laughter, the story about the revenant, that Baba Seck, eyes raised to the stars, told for my benefit while appearing to address the entire assembly:

"The last I heard, my niece, Maram Seck, succeeded in returning from an impossible land. And if that place is not death, it is at least adjacent to hell. She was abducted three years ago on the path that you take to come to Sor, Michel, when you travel here from the island of Saint-Louis. Back then, one did not require machetes to cut through the vegetation. There was no need to crawl under thickets; there were no thorns to scratch your skin. After Maram was abducted—by whom, we do not know—we let the path close up behind her. We abandoned it to the bush that protects us from kidnappers and slave traders.

"Maram was like you, Michel: she enjoyed solitude. From an early age, she would talk with animals and plants. She knew the secrets of the bush, and we do not know how it happened that this girl—who could hear us coming from a distance, who knew how to read signs—could have let herself be taken by surprise. I, Baba Seck, chief of the village of Sor, her mother's older brother, her only family since the death of her parents, I ran to Saint-Louis to find her. I questioned the *laptots* who go fishing on the river at dawn, the washerwomen, even the children of Saint-Louis who play by the water every day. I visited the prison of the fort; I questioned the guards. None of them had seen Maram.

"I was ready to pay her ransom, even if it meant selling myself to her captors, but they had disappeared before anyone could find out who they were or where they had come from. No doubt they had fled south without passing any of the nearby villages, because, despite the messengers that we sent in that direction, we discovered no trace of Maram. So it was that, three months after her disappearance, after beating the bush in every direction around the village to make sure she had not been taken by a lovelorn djinni in the form of a wild animal, we organized her funeral. I, Baba Seck, who should have married her to a healthy young man when the time came, I decided, since she had left without saying goodbye to us, that she would marry death. We wept, then we sang and danced for two days, as is our custom, to help her find serenity after the violence she had suffered, and so that she should leave us in peace, wherever she was, among the living or the dead.

"God is my witness that not a day has passed since then when I did not think about my niece, Maram Seck. And this is why we decided to close the path to Saint-Louis behind her, why we abandoned it to the bush. It is a tribute of inactivity that we pay to the bush so that it will defend us from kidnappers and slave traders."

Baba Seck fell silent then, and, like those who had known Maram Seck and were thinking about her, I meditated on what I had just heard. Who could have abducted her? Moorish horsemen coming from the right bank of the river would have been seen, as would warriors paid by African kings to ransack their own villages and abduct people to be sold as slaves to the Europeans. Had Baba Seck talked to the right people on the island of Saint-Louis? Had those people lied to him?

In unison with Baba Seck, who had been staring upward throughout his story, we raised our eyes to the stars, as if in those constellations we might discern the fates of the women and men on our Earth, as if our questions could be answered by looking up at the immensity of the universe.

I thought then, contemplating the African sky, that we counted for nothing, or almost nothing, in the universe. One must be in a state of some despair over its fathomless depths to imagine that any of our little actions, good or bad, could be weighed in the balance by an avenging God. That thought crossed my mind in more or less the same form as the one that you described to me, my dear Aglaé, during one of your recent visits to my home on rue de la Victoire. Beneath the stars of the village of Sor, listening to the story of Maram's mysterious disappearance told by her uncle Baba Seck, I had the sudden intuition that never in my life would I have enough intelligence to understand one millionth of the mysteries of our Earth. Far from paining me, however, the idea that I was nothing more than a grain of sand in the desert or a drop of water in the ocean exalted me. My mind had the power to locate my place, however minuscule it might be, amid that immensity. The awareness of my limits opened up infinity to me. I was now conscious dust, capable of thoughts as complex as the universe.

After a few moments of meditation, Baba Seck returned to his story. Everyone but Ndiak and myself had heard it before, but they all listened attentively even so.

"For three years we did not think about Maram. We had performed our last duties to her with a pain rendered more acute by our ignorance of her fate. But one fine morning, barely a month ago, a man came out of the bush. He was like you: tenacious enough to cut his own path through to us, indifferent to the thorns, brambles, and undergrowth that protect us. This man, who is one of the Serer people, is called Senghane Faye, and he told us he was a messenger from Maram, who had taken refuge in Ben, a village in Cap Vert, a peninsula not far from the island of Gorée. She had returned alive from beyond the seas, from that land where, for slaves, there is no return. Maram wanted to know if we had held her funeral. If so, she would never return to Sor and begged us not to try to find her because, if we did, a great misfortune would befall our village.

"Although we questioned Senghane Faye, Maram's envoy, he told us nothing else about her, nor why she had chosen him as her messenger. Although we begged him to tell us in detail about the fate of our daughter, Senghane Faye remained silent. Some of us, including my eldest son, were—and I understand them—astonished by his attitude, to the point that they doubted the veracity of his story. Why wouldn't he tell us more? What if he was an impostor who, having learned by chance of Maram Seck's disappearance, wanted to take advantage of the situation? But what advantage could he draw from such a message? Telling someone's relatives that they are alive when they are actually dead . . . isn't that an act of nameless cruelty?

"I had decided to escort him to the *kady* of Ndiébène, the king's representative, so that he could judge the case, but the morning after his arrival Senghane Faye—if that is his true name—disappeared, a little bit like Maram, leaving no trace. Since his disappearance, we do not know what to think of this man and his words about Maram. But there is one thing of which we are certain: his words have resurrected, in our thoughts and in our hearts, the hope that Maram really is alive."

XIII

". . . Returning to Senegal after being sold as a slave to the whites in America? That's as impossible as a circumcised man growing his foreskin back!"

Ndiak, who was fifteen now, mocked my interest in the story of the revenant as we made our way back to the island of Saint-Louis. It had all been invented by Baba Seck, he said. The villagers were laughing at me, Michel Adanson, the *toubab* who had swallowed all this nonsense. I would be a legend in their village.

"Ah, he's a clever man, that Baba Seck! He could swear a piece of the moon had fallen close to his village and you would believe him. But it's true that he speaks well."

I had already guessed that Ndiak was as curious as I was to discover the fate of the revenant when I told him my intention to sail to Cap Vert and find her. I knew how harshly Black slaves were treated in the Antilles and the Americas and I wondered how Maram's story could possibly be true. It was common to see colonists from the Antilles come back temporarily to France accompanied by some of their Black slaves to have them trained as coopers, carpenters, or blacksmiths, but no one had ever seen those slaves reappear in Africa, let alone their native village.

I knew, despite the nine years that separated Ndiak and myself, that we shared a youthful taste for adventure. On one hand, Ndiak was exaggerating his incredulity to encourage me to carry out my plan of going to the village of Ben to verify the existence of the revenant, despite the difficulties such a journey presented. On the other, Ndiak liked always being right, as do most people his age, and he was preparing a way out for himself in case we discovered when we got there that the story of the revenant was a mere fiction. But there were some obstacles blocking our more or less acknowledged desire to verify the existence of the revenant. The principal one was that I had only just returned from a journey to Cap Vert, and I was not supposed to go back to that region of Senegal before returning to France. The director general of the Concession, Estoupan de la Brüe, who had no respect for my botanical research, would never agree to provide men and resources to accompany me on a journey that had, in his eyes, no worthwhile purpose.

He and his brother, M. de Saint-Jean, the governor of Gorée, the island of slaves, did not like me. I had made it clear to them that I had absolutely no intention of working for the Concession as a clerk. They had hoped I would make up my mind to do this, in compensation for the expenses they had paid toward my research, after one of their better employees had died from a fever during a mission to the interior of Senegal. But I was not about to travel to every trading post on the river to barter muskets and gunpowder for ivory, gum arabic, or slaves. I was a botanist, an aspiring member of the Académie, not some clerk.

How, then, could I explain to them that I wished to go off in search of a Black woman who had supposedly returned from the Americas after three years of slavery, on the word of a story told by a Black village chief? The two brothers, both of them keen on the prospect of me going back to France, would laugh in my face. They would eagerly tell my protectors that I was causing harm to the Senegal Concession, whose most important trade—that of slaves—I would be accused of seeking to ruin. If the tale of the revenant were true, and I made it public, M. de la Brüe and M. de Saint-Jean would claim that I was disturbing the business of the King's Company, which at that time took in three to four million pounds a year from slavery.

Aware of my difficult relations with these two gentlemen of the Concession and supposing that I was at a dead end, Ndiak, who was struggling to conceal from me his desperate desire to discover the truth about the revenant, suggested to me a plan of action in the most casual, detached manner imaginable. I still recall vividly what he said. It cost him a great deal of effort not to laugh at his own impertinence.

"Adanson, I know in theory that children are not supposed to give advice to adults, but in this case I can't help it. If you truly wish to go to Cap Vert to verify the story of the revenant, you could tell M. de la Brüe, for example, that you have heard about a new species of very high-quality indigo growing on the island. Tell him it would be highly profitable for the Concession if you were allowed to go there in person to study it and collect a few specimens. You could even claim you need to observe the dyeing process used by the Africans in that region of Senegal. Adanson, this plan is very simple, and I am surprised that you, with all your science, didn't think of it on your own!"

I was accustomed to Ndiak's attempts to rouse me to anger. He had succeeded once and had immediately admitted to me, with an expression of delight, that he had taken a great deal of pleasure in seeing my eyes blaze and, above all, my cheeks and ears flush bright red. After that, he called me *Khonk Nop*, Red Ears, a nickname that stuck for quite a while. Consequently I forced myself to respond to his mockeries only with smiles, so as not to give him the joy of jeering as my face changed color. But, although his impertinence indisposed me against him, it did not make me rule out his strategy, which I had to acknowledge, to his great satisfaction, was not without its merits.

During my interview with Estoupan de la Brüe, a few days later in his office at the fort in Saint-Louis, in order to convince him to let me travel back to Cap Vert, I added another argument to those that Ndiak had suggested to me—an argument which gave me an anticipatory thrill at the idea of announcing it to my young companion and enraging him in turn. I argued that we could go from Saint-Louis to the village of Ben, in Cap Vert, not by boat but on foot.

For his part, M. de la Brüe suggested to me that it would be very useful for the Senegal Concession to gather recent data on the village of Meckhé, where the king of Kayor sometimes set up base with his entourage when he wished to deal personally in slaves not far from the Atlantic coast. This large fortified village, a little way inland, was more or less halfway between Saint-Louis and the Cap Vert peninsula, and it would be good, he said, if I could stop there. I agreed and M. de la Brüe told me, at the end of our interview, that he was granting me with immediate effect an escort of six armed men and two porters for my journey to Cap Vert.

"If you need more of anything when you get there, go and see my brother, Monsieur de Saint-Jean, on his island Gorée, and tell him I sent you."

M. de la Brüe was a pragmatic man who knew he could become something in the French East India Company—to which the Senegal Concession belonged—if he convinced its principal shareholders of his capacity to bring in large sums of money through an increase in the slave trade. When I met him then, in late August 1752, he was planning for my imminent return to France, and presumably he thought it necessary to keep up appearances as far as our relationship was concerned, which until then had been execrable.

He himself was back from a stay of almost two years in France, where he had been summoned to deal with certain family matters. His great-uncle Liliot-Antoine David, the governor general of the French East India Company, to whom my father had written to request support for my voyage to Senegal, must have implied to his great-nephew that he might be chosen as his successor. And indeed M. de la Brüe had not been the same since his return from Paris.

Whereas before he had made no attempt to hide from me, or from the clerks of the Senegal Commission, his taste for debauchery, he now sought to conceal it as much as possible. The troop of "unfortunate harlots" who escorted him everywhere he went—even when he was on a boat visiting all the slave-trading posts in the Concession, from Cap Blanc to the island of Bissau—had disappeared. He no longer loudly announced, to the amusement of his employees, who were just as debauched as he was, that he liked to explore the interior of Africa from top to bottom at least once every twelve hours. His licentiousness was no longer betrayed by his syphilitic, pockmarked face.

So it was a calculated decision by Estoupan de la Brüe not to cause me any difficulties but instead to grant me everything I needed for my overland journey from the island of Saint-Louis to the village of Ben, on the Cap Vert peninsula. Until then he had rudely refused all my requests for letters of safe-conduct, men, and resources that would have enabled me to set up makeshift offices where I could carry out my scientific experiments. He must have decided that his appointment to the highly coveted post of governor general of the French East India Company would be facilitated if he could demonstrate his detailed knowledge of Senegal's kings: their policies, their assets, their weaknesses. And in me, he thought he had found a useful informant.

Delighted by this softening of his attitude toward me, and guessing that I might have a hold over him, I agreed to become M. de la Brüe's spy. But the director of the Senegal Concession's hopes of promotion were ruined five years after my return to France, when the fort of Saint-Louis was taken by the English, with the fort on Gorée following suit a few months later.

Ndiak, whom I sought out just after my interview with M. de la Brüe, mistook the reason for my joyful expression. It was due in equal parts to the victory I believed I had won over the Concession director's avarice and to my anticipated satisfaction in seeing my young friend's face fall when I informed him that we would be walking, not sailing, to the village of Ben. It did not take long for this second reason to manifest itself. Ndiak smiled as I gave him time to revel in the glory of having had the idea of lying to Estoupan de la Brüe about the real reasons for our voyage, but his smile froze when I told him that we would be walking all along the coastline, probably for a period of several weeks. To my surprise and delight, he did not utter a single word of protest. What I didn't know then was that Ndiak was afraid for his life, but was too proud to admit it.

XIV

And so we left Saint-Louis on foot early in the morning of September 2, 1752, and, unlike Ndiak, I was happy. What I wrote in my published account of the voyage is not a lie: I hate ships. I suffered very badly from seasickness, and never discovered a remedy despite the many different ways I thought I had found to overcome it. There were ten of us: Ndiak, myself, two porters carrying my trunks—filled with instruments, books, and clothing—and six warriors from the kingdom of Waalo, armed with muskets. I did not mind at all that we advanced more slowly than we would have by sea.

We followed the inland road between Saint-Louis and the Cap Vert peninsula. It would have been quicker to go along the coastline, following the very long beach of pale sand that runs from Saint-Louis to the village of Yoff. But to carry out my espionage mission on the villages belonging to the king of Kayor, I had planned to cut across the roads that joined them from the east. Estoupan de la Brüe had granted us a letter of safe-conduct that ensured our relative safety on this route, which was punctuated by freshwater wells where we could quench our thirst quite regularly. Not only that—and this was important for me—but the species of plants and animals were more varied and less well-known inland than they were on the Atlantic coast.

Our departure from Saint-Louis was slow. We were in no rush, as if we wanted to delay the moment of our hypothetical encounter with the revenant. As long as we had not yet seen her, there was a chance that she existed. So, distracted by all the wonders of nature that are so abundant in Senegal, Ndiak and I did not hesitate to stray from the path to follow a distant herd of elephants or to track, always from a distance, a pack of lions.

Ndiak was no less patient than I was. I had instructed him in the methods of natural history at more or less the same age I myself had been when, with my father's blessing, I first developed a passion for the subject. My young friend was constantly drawing my attention to specimens that he thought would be interesting for me to observe, or that he believed I should sketch, or that he feared I might not notice. It was he who remarked—in the middle of a small stretch of deep water that the people of that land call a *marigot* and which we were walking alongside at that moment—a wonderfully beautiful plant known as the *Cadelari*. Its leaves in the sunlight glimmered like silver silk, or like downy feathers shimmering with water and light. Ndiak gestured to it, his eyelids blinking as he tried not to laugh. Since I couldn't swim and did not want to get wet, he foresaw that I would have no end of trouble in collecting a specimen of this aquatic plant. We stopped on the shore, with the plant about twenty *toises* away from us. I estimated that the *marigot* was not too deep and that, if I perched on the shoulders of one of our porters, a Bambara man who was just over six feet tall, I perhaps had a chance of collecting the *Cadelari*. I took off my frock coat and my shoes and I climbed onto the porter's back. He was neck-deep in the water before we were even halfway to my plant. He was a courageous man, however, and did not stop walking even when his head disappeared underwater. I myself was half-submerged by the time I managed to catch hold of the *Cadelari* with my fingertips. Busy with this delicate task, I forgot that my Bambara porter, whose name was Kélitigui, would probably need to breathe very soon, and that my passion for this plant might well see the pair of us drown. But Kélitigui was a force of nature and, having sensed from my movements on his shoulders that I was now in possession of my treasure, walked slowly and smoothly back to shore, as if he had suddenly grown gills and become an amphibian. Back on dry land, he set me down as if I were nothing more than a small parcel. He did not appear distressed, or at least he was trying not to show it. To reward him, I gave him a leather purse, which he immediately hung around his neck. Ndiak was no longer laughing with his eyes or blinking furiously; he looked appalled. I was as proud of the effect I had produced upon my young friend as I was of my plant.

Since we were still not far from Saint-Louis, despite having walked for two days, we began to hunt waterfowl. I shot down a few woodcocks, and the occasional teal or duckling, birds that—like our European swallows—come to this part of Africa to escape the winter. In the evening we roasted them, sharing them with our companions, along with some wild fruit collected along the way. I had a predilection for *ditakh*, a small round fruit unknown in Europe, inside whose walnut-colored exterior—a little harder than the shell of a boiled egg—is hidden a floury, bright green flesh, interlaced with white fibers around a pit. When sucked, the fibers of this pit released sap that tasted both sweet and slightly acid. This fruit not only filled me up but quenched my thirst too, so I consumed a large number of them during our journey. Sometimes, even today, the taste of *ditakh* comes alive on my tongue when I think about my secret voyage in Senegal.

It was not until we left Ndiébène, the first village on the coastline that once belonged to the king of Kayor, that Ndiak and I forced ourselves to walk at a faster pace.

In the evenings, when we didn't stop at a village, our porters would set up camp and our six warriors—all of them Waalo-Waalos, like Ndiak—would guard it throughout the night. Because while the route we were taking was beautiful, and offered fascinating opportunities for botanical research, it was also dangerous. We quickly realized this from the fear on the faces of the peasants who ran to take refuge in the bush at our approach. Seeing our muskets, they thought we must be slave hunters, out on a *moyäl*—a raid—like the mercenaries paid by the king of Kayor, or those of his eastern neighbor in the kingdom of Jolof.

Rare were the peasants who offered us hospitality. The state of perpetual war at the time in that kingdom brought famine to lands where nourishing cereals such as millet and sorghum grew very easily. But the madness of that country's kings, like those of kings all over the world, does not veil from them the necessity of feeding their people, if only so they can continue ruling over the living. As Ndiak told me sententiously, his eyes blinking furiously, the index finger of his right hand raised: "The dead are not beautiful, they don't work, and they don't pay taxes. So they are no use at all to kings."

Consequently, certain villages were spared the raids. Better protected, more prosperous than others, they assured their survival—as well as that of smaller hamlets in their constituency—by cultivating the land. It was in one of these little villages where raids were more or less forbidden that I had an adventure which cheered Ndiak up for the first time during our voyage.

At dawn we left the camp we had set up the previous night, not far from a hamlet named Tiari, and before noon we aimed to reach the village of Lompoul, located to the south of a narrow strip of desert that looked like a stray fragment of the Sahara: the same dunes of white or reddish sand, their color depending on the strength of the wind and the position of the sun in the sky; the same fear of getting lost and dying of thirst even if the desert's width, from the Atlantic shoreline to its easternmost borders, did not exceed two or three leagues.

We were racing against time. From daybreak on, the heat would mount with extraordinary rapidity, frightening even the Senegalese. Whatever happened, we had to reach the village of Lompoul before the hour when, to use Ndiak's words, "the sun eats the shadows"—in other words, when the sun hangs directly above the Earth and burns it pitilessly.

"Originally we were white," added Ndiak. "It was from having the sun directly over our heads that we became black. One especially hot day, the shadows, hunted by the sun, took refuge in our skin."

After two hours, pounded by a rain of burning light, the sand of the dunes where we walked began to boil. I sank my

feet into this sea of fire, where my shoes felt as heavy as those
of a suicidal man who ties a weight to his ankle to help him
drown. A glint of red was beginning to appear on Ndiak's
black face, so I guessed that mine must be scarlet. This time,
however, Ndiak was suffering so much, despite his dark skin
which was supposed to offer protection from the sun, that
the thought of mocking me did not cross his mind. I could
feel my cheeks cooking under my hat. The sweat that trickled
down my neck had dried on my back before it reached the
bottom of my shirt. I had already taken off my light cotton
coat, unable to bear the weight of it on my shoulders. But I
soon put it back on because I had the impression that another
layer of fabric would better shield me from the flames that
poured straight down from above. We were dying of thirst
even though we kept drinking. Kept in goatskins, the sun-
warmed water was not enough to refresh us. I thought I had
found a solution in a *ditakh*, sucking the floury flesh and mix-
ing it with saliva, but every time I opened my mouth I would
swallow gulps of hot air that dried my tongue and set fire to
the back of my throat.

When we reached Lompoul, there was still a small shadow
faithfully clinging to our feet. The sun had not yet poured
down on our heads all its reserves of heat. We rushed over to
the well. The chief of the village, whom we had barely greeted,
ordered his men to help us draw cool water. Used to people
arriving from the neighboring desert in a feverish state, the
old man guided us to the shade of a straw canopy big enough
to shelter us all, along with a host of curious villagers. The
coolness of the shade in that spot seemed so overwhelming to
us that we were almost shivering with cold. Our skin secreted

torrents of sweat, after all the water we had drunk. I had not yet removed my hat to greet the chief of Lompoul, but once I was in the shade I did so. The crowd of villagers watched as I exposed the drenched hair at my temples and a black line running across my forehead, left by the dye in my hat. Ndiak, who blamed me for all the suffering brought on by this sweltering journey, suddenly burst out laughing when he saw me bare-headed:

"Adanson, you're wearing your share of shadow in the middle of your forehead. If we'd had to walk another hour through the Lompoul Desert, you would be as black as us!"

Everyone started laughing and I opted to smile to save myself from further teasing. Ndiak did not know how true his words were when he talked about my share of shadow. While that black stripe was only superficial, it seems to me that it must have infected my blood with a melancholy that has never truly left me since that wretched voyage. I did not know that yet, however, and, to thank our hosts for their generous welcome—they had also given us millet couscous, washed down with camel's milk—I decided to theatrically untie my hair, which was very long at that time, before their curious eyes.

I was sitting cross-legged on a mat, surrounded by all those villagers, and, aware that I was being observed as the representative of a race little-known by the Africans of that region, I slowly untied the leather queue bag that held my hair prisoner at the base of my neck and shook my head so that it would fall loose over my shoulders. Head lowered, I stared through my fringe at the children in front of me. The youngest among them, who saw me as a frightening beast, nevertheless appeared tempted to approach me. One brave little boy, no more than a year old, suddenly escaped his older sister's arms. She cried out in alarm, but did not dare go after him. Completely naked, with a leather charm tied around his neck, the boy—after taking a dozen unsteady steps—grabbed a handful of my hair to stop himself falling. If there is one people in the world that most loves small children, it is undoubtedly the Senegalese. So I won the hearts of all the villagers when, after delicately loosening the toddler's fists and releasing the two thick locks of my hair he had been gripping, I sat up straight, having previously been leaning toward him, and threw my head back, sweeping my mane along with it. In the same movement, I sat the child down very close to me, facing in my direction, and took his right hand in mine to ask all the customary questions that two adults address to each other when they meet. I parodied those greetings to make the villagers laugh:

"What is your family name? Has anything bad happened to you? Is your life peaceful? May peace be upon your home. For myself, thanks be to God, I am fine. How is your father? How is your mother? And how are your children? And your big sister, who was screaming with terror just now when you escaped her arms to come and touch my hair, has she recovered?"

I am not a naturally funny man, but I felt like one that day, particularly since the little boy, who was staring at me and who had not yet learned to speak, was babbling a few syllables in an identical tone to mine, as if genuinely trying to reply to all my questions.

So it was that my new little friend and I brought tears of laughter to all the surrounding eyes. And the looks of affection and friendship that greeted me throughout the rest of our short stay in the village of Lompoul proved to me once again that the natives of Senegal are neither savage nor blood-thirsty, but wonderfully good-natured.

As I write this to you now as an old man, Aglaé, my heart aches at the idea that that little child—whose name, Makhou, has suddenly come to me—was perhaps kidnapped during the troubled period that struck the area around Lompoul after my voyage to Senegal. What was he told about me, the first *toubab* he ever met? Did his parents, or his older sister, have time to describe our madcap conversation to him? Is he, at this moment, still surrounded by his family in the village of Lompoul or has he become a slave in the Americas? Does he have grand-children to whom he enjoys telling the story of our meeting, his lips curled into a smile, or is he chained up and thinking, as he curses my race, that I presaged the ruin of his life?

With the passing of time, my dear Aglaé, the joys and sufferings of our existence are intermingled until they have the bittersweet flavor of the forbidden fruit in the Garden of Eden.

XV

When we left the village of Lompoul we did not head south
as we should have to reach Cap Vert by the quickest route, but
took a more easterly path. When I explained to Ndiak that we
were going to Meckhé, the second-largest stronghold in the
kingdom of Kayor after Mboul, his expression changed but
he said nothing. I peppered him with questions and at last he
admitted to me that, in choosing to go to Meckhé, I was reck-
lessly leading him and our escort into danger. Had I forgotten
that he was a son of the king of Waalo? Didn't I know that his
father, Ndiak Aram Bocar, had waged war against the king
of Kayor, in a battle in which many warriors lost their lives?
It was true that I knew the king of Kayor had lost the Battle
of Ndob, just before my arrival in Senegal in 1749, ceding the
neighboring village of Ndiébène, not far from the fort on the
island of Saint-Louis. But, despite Ndiak's legitimate qualms,
I felt compelled to keep the promise I had made to the director of the Senegal Concession to gather information on
Meckhé, its precise location, the number of its inhabitants,
the size of the royal court and the king's army. This had been
the price I had agreed to pay for permission to return to Cap
Vert for a reason I had not been able to reveal to M. de la Brüe:

to find the revenant and hear her story. Ndiak was, therefore, in the uncomfortable position of being the trickster who had himself been fooled. I felt guilty at hiding this from him, but I had no other choice but to leave him in ignorance of the deal I had struck with the Concession's director.

It was our good chance that, following his defeat at the Battle of Ndob, the former king of Kayor had been deposed. In his place, Mam Bathio Samb had been elected king by a college of seven wise men gathered in Mboul. In reality, though, Mam Bathio Samb did not owe his election to this vote. He had been secretly installed as *damel* of Kayor by the king of Waalo, Ndiak's father. Ndiak himself knew no more about this arrangement than I did. We would discover it together in Meckhé, quickly relieving our anxieties about what fate might have in store for us there.

After a brisk two-day walk, we arrived in Meckhé to find the village in a state of great agitation. We came to the conclusion that the king's armed men had let us pass along the road to Meckhé—including me, the white who ought to have aroused suspicion—because they believed we were going there to attend King Mam Bathio Samb's wedding.

Quickly realizing that it was in our interests to pretend that we had strayed from the route to Cap Vert to celebrate these nuptials, we were taken in charge at the northern entrance to the village by a local chief who led us to our place of residence. This was an enclosure of five huts surrounded by a fence the height of a man, where the chief ordered us to be provided with jugs of cool water to revive us after our journey. I was not surprised by this act of hospitality generally known as *téranga*, which is a virtue shared among almost all the Senegalese. But it was possible that all this attentiveness indicated that the local chief had been expecting us. The king's spies must have warned him in advance of the intention of the *toubab* to enter Meckhé with his escort. I felt sure of this when, as we were finishing up the water, a handsome and powerful man entered our enclosure, followed by two warriors armed with long buccaneer guns.

Unlike the local chief, this man, who wore a red headdress of a similar shape to our Phrygian caps, did not remove it in my presence—a way of making me understand that he was not my inferior. I kept my own hat elegantly upon my head—my hat which had suffered greatly during our crossing of the Lompoul Desert—and asked him as politely as possible to sit down on a large mat that I'd had unrolled on the fine sand of our courtyard. In contrast to Baba Seck, the chief of the village of Sor, who, even though we became friends, always sat at the very edge of the mat we shared since I was French, this man sat facing me and, looking straight into my eyes, pronounced these words, which I recall even now, so deeply did they mark me:

"My name is Malaye Dieng. In the name of our King Mam Bathio Samb, I thank you, Michel Adanson, for accompanying Ndiak, son of the king of Waalo, our ally Ndiak Aram Bocar, to Meckhé to attend the king's wedding."

Stunned, I stammered a few words of thanks on behalf of all of us, while imagining young Ndiak standing behind me, trying not to laugh. So it wasn't Ndiak who was in my service, but I who was in his! In a single phrase I had become the equivalent of the courtier facing me, merely one more member of Prince Ndiak's escort. I immediately wondered how the king of Kayor's envoy knew our names. Had we been identified as soon as we set off from the island of Saint-Louis, while we had blithely imagined that Ndiak's origins would remain a secret throughout our journey?

Malaye Dieng took his leave by inviting us, on behalf of the king of Kayor, to attend part of the festivities the next morning; he would come to fetch us after the second prayer of the day. Once I had accompanied him to the door of our enclosure, as required by protocol, and after he had bade me farewell in turn, I came back into the courtyard, where I saw Ndiak sitting cross-legged in the center of the mat. His back straight, blinking furiously to stop himself from laughing, this fifteen-year-old boy looked me up and down imperiously: he was playing the part of king. I decided to push him over the edge of his hilarity by sitting modestly in a corner of the mat and obsequiously removing my hat. This was enough to send the members of our escort—the armed guards as well as our porters—into hysterics. For the first and last time during our voyage, Ndiak cried with laughter.

A man with many wives already, the king of Kayor was marrying a Laobé woman in order to gain, so it was said, the secret powers over the trees and animals of the bush possessed by leaders of her people. Unlike our kings and emperors in Europe, the kings of Senegal have no fear of misalliances. So, while it was forbidden for a member of the nobility in that land to marry someone in order to access the hidden powers of his wife's caste, no such prohibition existed for kings.

"The Laobés are bush-clearers," Ndiak explained. "It is they who enable kingdoms to extend their arable land. They know the prayers that must be recited before cutting down trees, as well as all the precautions to be taken to remove all the village's genies from the bush. Without the Laobés, kings would not be able to find new lands to distribute to their courtiers and soldiers."

I was still a young man then, and, although I hardly ever thought twice about saying what was on my mind, in this instance I forced myself not to reply to Ndiak that this imagined power over supposed occult forces was nothing but a crude superstition. Now that I am old, however, I see in these beliefs one of the wonderful subterfuges used by other societies to prevent men from despoiling nature. Despite my Cartesianism, my faith in the omnipotence of reason, as celebrated by the philosophers whose ideals I shared, I like to imagine that the women and men of that dry land know how to speak to trees and ask their forgiveness before cutting them down. Trees are alive, just as we are, and if it is true that we had to make ourselves masters and possessors of Mother Nature, we should have scruples about exploiting her with no regard for her feelings. I no longer find it absurd, now that I have greater experience of life, that men of a different race from mine should have a representation of the world that shows a respect for the lives of trees.

In the ebony forests that once filled the sixty leagues of coastline separating the Cap Vert peninsula from the island of Saint-Louis, very few trees remain. Chopped down in vast quantities by Europeans during the two centuries preceding my voyage to Senegal, they can now be seen in the marquetry of our writing desks, our cabinets of curiosities, the keys of our harpsichords. They are displayed or hidden in the choirs of our cathedrals, in the sculpted details of so many organ cases, stalls, pulpits, and confessionals. One day, moved by a sort of animism while standing before the deep black wood of an altarpiece, it occurred to me that if the pagan prayers of a Laobé sage had been required for each tree cut down, the great ebony forest might not yet have disappeared from Senegal. And so, kneeling in that dark church, surrounded by their nailed and varnished corpses, I began to pray to the ebony trees to forgive the sins of those who had chopped, sawed, and transported them to this place under another sky, so far from their mother Africa.

XVI

Meckhé was a fortified village surrounded by high fences that enclosed a very large number of huts. There too, although no doubt with the consent of the Laobés, nature had been forced to pay a costly tribute in wood to men. Ndiak had explained to me that it had been a war chief, the Farba Kaba, who had incited all his enemies to follow his example by erecting spiked fences to protect certain villages from the *moyäl*. He also made clear to me that the meetings of royal advisers to plan a war or a raid—those meetings known as *lël*—generally took place in warrior villages such as Meckhé.

It seemed almost certain that we were under surveillance. While in all the villages we had gone through before, the whiteness of my skin had been an attraction, here, nobody—not even a child—hid behind the fences of our enclosure to spy upon us. And, after the departure of Malaye Dieng, no matter how hard I tried to start conversations with the people I met on the way to the market, I got little reward for my efforts. To the general questions I asked about how often the market was held, or the number of people who lived in Meckhé, all I received in response were polite smiles and evasive answers. Fearing that they would start to suspect I really was a spy, I contented myself with estimating the population and size of Meckhé.

Free to wander around, I counted more than two hundred fires, which suggested that the village's population was roughly eighteen hundred souls—in other words just over half the population of the island of Saint-Louis. Each neighborhood in this stronghold appeared to have its own well, meaning Meckhé could sustain a siege of several weeks without running out of water. On the large central square, the vast market overflowed with fruit, vegetables, cereals, spices, dried fish, and meat from the bush or from farms. The surrounding hamlets had seemed to me on the verge of famine, but now I understood that all the resources in this region of the kingdom of Kayor were directed toward Meckhé. I did not know if this information might be useful to Estoupan de la Brüe. I promised myself I would pass it on to him, but—as you will read, Aglaé, in the account that follows in these notebooks—the director of the Concession never asked me to provide him with a written report of my last voyage to Cap Vert.

XVII

The next morning, after the second prayer of the day, the messenger Malaye Dieng came as promised to fetch us. In honor of the king of Kayor, we were dressed in our finest clothes. I had changed my outfit and wore cream-colored breeches that matched my frock coat. I had traded my old shoes, destroyed by the heat of the Lompoul Desert, for a pair of sheepskin slippers and had their buckles shined. My hair was tied in a ponytail, held in place by a black velvet bow, and on my head I wore a black tricorn hat, which, like all my clean clothes, came from a trunk carried by one of our porters. Ndiak, who also had a small trunk packed with clothes, had put on a pair of baggy yellow cotton pants. Above this he wore a shirt dyed indigo, its collar embroidered with gold thread, open on the sides and tightened at the waist with a wide strip of fabric the same color as his pants. His yellow leather boots had pointed toes and came all the way up to the middle of his thigh: his way of showing that he was a good horseman of noble blood. The hat he wore, tied under his chin, was the same cotton Phrygian cap as that worn by the king of Kayor's envoy, except that it was dark yellow and decorated with more cowries—the little shells that could be used as money among the Senegalese.

Proud that he rather than I was the king's guest of honor, Ndiak walked as slowly as possible ahead of us, frowning as he turned his head from side to side, his nose raised to the wind. As for myself, in the labyrinth of Meckhé's narrow, sandy streets, I continued to count the wells I saw. There were three on the path we took, though there was nothing around them, in contrast to the wells I had seen the previous day.

Long before we reached the village's southern gate— through which we entered a large, square plain, its edges lined by several hundred villagers all standing pressed together—we had begun to hear the continual rumble of fourteen *sabar*: drums of various sizes. I was almost dazed by the din they made as we passed close to them to reach, on the other side of the square, facing the gate we had just come through, the vast royal canopy, under which the messenger indicated we should sit, not far behind two carved wooden thrones.

The sound of those drums was so powerful that, in their proximity, I felt as if my guts were twisted and that the rhythm of my heartbeat was forced into time with theirs. About one-third of those drums gave a heavy, deep sound while the other two-thirds responded in a higher tone, but the drum played by the band's leader, who looked to me to be the oldest of the drummers, made a sound like the crackle of torrential rain. There was nothing extraordinary about the appearance of this drummer, who in the fashion of that land wore a blue and white cotton shirt open on the sides, but he abused the skin of his instrument with such vigorous dexterity that I had the impression that the sounds produced by his *sabar* stood out from those of all the others, even while continuing to be supported by them, the way an old man might intermittently press down with his cane on the ground to stop himself falling. The hail-like noise of his drum would suddenly explode, interspersed with silence, before setting off again on its wild, staggering trajectory.

In addition to the fourteen drums, two young people were running in all directions around the square to amuse the crowd. They played *tamas*, held in place by straps that went over their shoulders and under their left armpits, and they struck the skin sometimes with the left hand, balled in a fist, and sometimes with the right hand, with the aid of a small piece of wood curved at a right angle. The sound produced could be made higher or lower depending on the pressure they exerted with the inside of their left bicep on strings that tensed or slackened the skin, which they battered with sharp little blows. They must have been a little like the king's jesters, because they wore a serene smile on their faces while pressing their chins into their necks, with one of their legs always in the air, their left arm flapping like a withered wing. It was as if they were mimicking those tall wading birds on the banks of the Senegal River who, when they grow sleepy and take a rest on one of their two spindly legs, head sheltered under a wing, abruptly unfold the other wing so they don't lose their balance.

Ndiak and I were positioned among the most important nobles in the kingdom, while the rest of our troop had been placed farther back, to the side of the royal canopy. As we made our way through the dignitaries sitting on the ground, I could feel the weight of their eyes upon me. They barely responded to our greetings, quickly turning away so that no one could say they were watching us.

Soon after we sat down on beautiful mats of woven rushes, emitting a pleasant scent of cut roses, the fourteen drums fell silent. Heralded by a griot shouting praises at the top of his voice, the king advanced slowly on horseback. Both he and his mount were protected from the heat by a red cotton sunshade, fringed with a golden braid, its long handle supported by a servant dressed entirely in white.

A tall man, the king wore a sky-blue cotton tunic, open on the sides, the fabric of which was so starched that it looked as rigid and shiny as a suit of armor. A yellow silk scarf decorated with gold tassels was tied around his waist, and the pointed toes of his high yellow leather boots, like those of Moroccan sandals, poked through the long stirrups. On his head he wore a bloodred felt hat, also decorated with a gold tassel, which hung down over his right shoulder and sparkled like a star whenever a ray of sunlight touched it.

The horse ridden by the king was a Senegal Barbary, its dapple-gray coat accentuated by the contrast with the dark red leather saddle and the reins of the same color that he held in his right hand. A large talisman in red leather identical to that of the saddle and the reins covered the animal's chest, partly concealing a wide scar of exposed pink flesh, presumably the mark left by an old battle wound. Yellow and midnight-blue wool pompoms decorated the horse's chamfron. It wore no blinkers. From time to time, the king caressed its neck with his left hand.

The bride followed, also on horseback. Her head and shoulders were covered by a white pagne richly adorned with gold coins. From what Ndiak explained to me, I gathered that when the king had reached the enclosure where his future wife was waiting for him, he had had to pick her out from among several young women whose heads had also been covered with pagnes. Since tradition had it that the couple would be happy if the groom identified his spouse correctly, she had no doubt chosen the opulently decorated pagne that still covered her head to distinguish her from the others, making his task easier.

The bride's horse was the same dapple-gray color and had the same harness as the king's. But its reins were held by an imposing woman wearing a white cotton dress, her head girded with the same fabric, who must have been the bride's eldest aunt.

Once the royal couple had been installed under the canopy, the fourteen drums were pounded once again.

Ndiak and I were behind the king and queen. They sat as straight as they could on low seats that appeared, from my viewpoint, to be uncomfortable, if beautiful. I do not remember now all the details of those little sculpted thrones, but I do know that they had been carved in the bride's honor by Laobé artisans, renowned for their skill in woodwork. The name of the king's new wife was Adjaratou Fam, and King Mam Bathio Samb was marrying her to win over the leader of her caste. The Malaw Fam was the bride's father and was reputed to have such mastery of the secrets of wood that he could sculpt statuettes that on moonless nights could move around on their own to commit murder at his command.

I did not believe such tales, but they did show to me that wherever men seek to remain in power, they will always find stratagems to inspire terror in their inferiors. Though a result of their power, the fear they inspire in others is proportional to their own fear of losing that power. The greater their power, the more terrible their terror. The Malaw Fam must have been enviably powerful indeed to feel the need to surround himself with such deadly mysteries. And he must have been a skillful and cunning man, since, however despised his caste might be by the country's nobility, the king of Kayor had not hesitated to marry his daughter in order to make him his ally.

The Laobés, as I learned after the festivities, were renowned not only for their miracles of woodwork but also for their art as dancers. In all the years since that wedding, I have never seen such shameless poses as those struck by the Laobés. Following the rhythm of the drums, a dozen women lined up facing the same number of men. Emerging one after another from their respective lines, they formed couples in the middle of the dancing area. They would then mime—frenetically, but still in rhythm—the act of love for as long as the bandleader desired, before returning to their lines upon his order. And this handsome spectacle ended when, in a single movement, the two groups of dancers approached one another again, practically thigh to thigh, to the point that I seemed to be seeing an intermingling of arms and legs thrown in the air amid a cloud of ocher dust.

I have often seen mimes at the Saint-Germain Fair in Paris, and have noticed that when they pretend to fall or receive blows from a stick, or other such mummeries, they do so in such an exaggerated way that their actions appear grotesque to the public. This thought led me, seeing the Laobés imitating the act of love in their frenetic dance, to consider the possibility that it might after all be a legitimate means of amusing the public. But I must admit that, being unused to this kind of theater, the effect it had upon me was far from comical. In that dance, called the *Leumbeul*, the swaying of the women's hips is so perfectly matched to the rhythm of the drums that one ends up believing that the true conductor of this diabolical spectacle is their behinds. I confess that I was moved by the vision of all those callipygian Venuses dancing like she-devils.

If the new bride's people had dominated the early part of the festivities, it was now the turn of the king of Kayor, who commanded his horses to dance. At first I did not understand why a group of ten horsemen was slowly approaching the drums. Each of them was richly dressed, and I had the impression that the color of their clothing was deliberately matched to the pagnes tied to their saddles, which covered their legs and floated over the flanks of their horses. Generally sunshine-yellow, indigo, or ocher, these pagnes shared by the rider and his mount made me feel, through a sort of optical illusion amplified by the blinding dazzle of sunlight on sand, that what I was seeing were centaurs—those fabulous beings of the Ancient World, half man, half horse. This illusion grew stronger when the riders began to dance, one after another, a few steps away from the king and his new bride.

From where Ndiak and I were sitting, the high headdresses worn by king and queen intermittently blocked our view. And it seemed to me that the riders' chests took the place of their horses' heads and that their legs, hidden by the pagnes, became horses' legs. The riders, arms raised to the sky, guided their mounts so discreetly that I could have sworn that the creatures I saw rearing up before us, making the sand fly rhythmically under their hooves, were not men but smiling, giant centaurs. When the horses began to dance in unison, the high-pitched cries of the crowd grew so loud that they almost drowned out the racket of those fourteen drummers who were hammering the skins of their instruments without any signs of fatigue, despite the heat of the sun that had been beating down on us for several hours.

At an invisible sign from the king to his chamberlain, all noise was suddenly extinguished. And in the silence that followed the deafening din of the horse dance, the rumble of drums continued to resonate so loudly inside my head that I felt as if my neighbors could hear the sound pouring from my ears. But it was probably just the beating of my heart that, having matched itself to the unchanging rhythm of the deepest drums, prolonged their rumble in my mind. Even now sometimes, hearing my heart in the silence of an insomniac night, I believe that I can hear the overpowering rhythm of those drums in Meckhé, played in honor of the king of Kayor and his new bride, Adjaratou Fam.

The king and his last queen remounted their dapple-gray horses. Preceded by their griots, who once again began bellowing praises, they returned to their palatial enclosure hidden among a maze of alleys, known only to their inner circle. As soon as they had disappeared behind the southern gate of the village, through which they had arrived at the start of the ceremony, the main square became the site of a gigantic sacrificial ceremony: twenty-one white, black, and red bulls were killed in accordance with long and complex rituals that I did not understand. It was not until nightfall that I saw the meat roasting above wide, glowing red fires that blazed up from pits dug in the sand—the very same sand where men, women, and horses had danced only a few hours before. Skewered on spears held up at their ends by long, knotty stakes, they dripped fat onto the flames below, sending them into ecstatic dances.

Later, our bellies full of the grilled meat sliced up and served in calabashes, our thirst quenched by pints of palm wine served by the king's slaves, we returned to our enclosure. Behind us, the last clouds of smoke, fragrant with the burned fat of the sacrificed animals, rose into the sky above the bush. And all night long we heard the hyenas, lions, and panthers beyond the village fortifications, fighting over the carcasses of the twenty-one bulls with which the king had gratified his two peoples: first, the men and women of the village, and next, the creatures of the bush, offered to him as a dowry by the Laobés.

XVIII

The next day, the king of Kayor, to thank Ndiak, the son of the king of Waalo, for having honored his wedding with his presence, and to thank me for having escorted him there, arranged for each of us to be presented, by the king's messenger, Malaye Dieng, with a young, dark bay Senegal Barbary. These two horses, which must have been brothers, since they both had the same white crescent-shaped markings between their eyes, were given to us equipped with saddles. But I was intrigued by Ndiak's saddle. It was very different from mine, which resembled all the others I had seen the previous day, in red or dark yellow leather, inlaid with silver floral arabesques in a Moorish style. I concealed my curiosity, however, deciding I would examine it more closely later.

After warmly thanking Malaye Dieng, Ndiak handed him our gift in exchange. In the hope that it would allay any suspicions they might have that I was a spy for the Senegal Concession, and despite its relative modesty, I had suggested to Ndiak that we offer the king one of the two watches I had bought from Caron, the most famous watchmaker in Paris, just before my departure for Africa. It was Ndiak who gave the king's envoy the more finely worked of the two watches, telling him, as I had explained, that the king of France and his sisters possessed identical models. Malaye Dieng took his leave of us once Ndiak had shown him the workings of this watch, whose new precision mechanism had been a succès d'estime at Versailles. This object was fashionable at the Court back when the younger Caron—long before he became Beaumarchais—was famous only for the inventions he dreamed up in his father's watchmaking workshop.

Tactfully, Ndiak offered Malaye Dieng a gift on behalf of both of us—a curved dagger with an ivory pommel, and a leather sheath inlaid with silver thread—to thank him for his assistance. Then we accompanied him to the door of our enclosure, where, in accordance with the customs of the Senegalese, we repeated our thanks and farewells before he finally left. As soon as his back was turned, Ndiak ran to our two horses, which were tied to the trunk of a mango tree in the middle of the courtyard. The horses were twins but, as I have already mentioned, their saddles were not identical, and—ignoring the protests of Ndiak, who was eager to ride his new mount—I had his saddle removed so I could examine it at my ease.

This saddle had the brown leather backrest and the three straps joined by a buckle under the animal's belly characteristic of English saddle-making. Although I could not be sure, I sensed that the gift of this English saddle to Ndiak might have been meant as a secret message for me, or even for the director of the Senegal Concession. Was it possible that the king of Kayor was suggesting that he could, if he wished, or if he considered it advantageous, offer preferential treatment to the English rather than the French? Offered as it was to the son of a traditional ally of the French, this gift seemed to me more eloquent than a long political speech. I thought it was time to inform Ndiak about my arrangement with M. de la Brüe so that he would not be exposed to his father's reproaches when the king of Waalo saw this English saddle. I did not want him to think he had been duped by me throughout our voyage. I considered him my friend.

It was only once we had left Meckhé and were on the road to Keur Damel, a village on the Atlantic coast where the king of Kayor sometimes went to negotiate with the French—and, apparently, with the English too—that I revealed the truth to Ndiak. He merely laughed and said he had always suspected that I had some connection with the Senegal Concession, even though I was not their employee. He found it natural that Estoupan de la Brüe should have asked me to spy on all the kingdoms in northern Senegal. And, since we were confiding in each other, he added that he had been spying on me from the beginning on behalf of his father, the king of Waalo, but that I shouldn't worry: I could count on him to keep my secrets. He didn't tell his father everything, only certain details.

I was unsure what to make of his frankness. I didn't know if he was joking as usual or if it was true that he was his father's spy. It seemed strange to me that such a young man—he had been only twelve when M. de la Brüe had brought us together—should have been entrusted with such an important mission. But the remainder of our unfortunate voyage showed me that Ndiak, despite his youth and his mischievous nature, was genuinely attached to me.

For now, he was so happy and so proud of the horse with

its English saddle given to him by the king of Kayor that he kept urging the beast into a gallop, on the road that led us to the next stage of our journey, merely for the pleasure of speed. And while the cloud of dust that he left behind him would make me think that I would not see my friend again for a long time, we would always find him within half a league, standing beside the animal and caressing its neck or checking its legs and its horseshoes, making sure of the horse's well-being. After a third impromptu stop, when we found him offering the animal water poured from his own gourd into the hollow of his joined hands, I persuaded him that if he continued at this rate, his horse would undoubtedly become ill.

"Or, worse still," I added, "you might lose his respect. An animal bred for racing like yours must have good reasons to gallop. If not, he will not obey you when you actually need him to move fast. You stop so often to look after him that there is a risk he will take such affectionate whims for granted. And if you spoil a horse, you will never be able to undo the harm."

My words hit their mark. Ndiak was so proud of his rank that he decided he ought to listen to me to avoid the possibility that he might one day lose face with his "equals"—by which he meant the men, women, and children of the royal family to which he belonged. From a very young age, he had, like certain nobles in the ancien régime, been taught by his entourage not to suffer any public affront without immediately seeking to remedy it, even at the cost of his own life. If someone disrespected him, it was not only his own honor at stake, but the honor of his entire family.

"You're right, Adanson—my horse should not behave

ridiculously because he now belongs to my clan. Moreover, even though he is a stallion, I am going to name him after the person I love most in the world—my mother, Mapenda Fall."

"As for myself," I replied, "I will not name my horse after my mother."

"Why, don't you love her?" Ndiak asked.

"I do. But I do not love this animal enough to give it my mother's name."

"Then it will be a horse with no name," concluded Ndiak, clearly unfazed by my barb.

Having pronounced these words in a pompous tone, Ndiak rode his horse slowly, very close to mine. After a few minutes of silence, he began trying to convince me to change our route.

"Apart from the watch we gave him, the greatest gift we could offer the king of Kayor is not to ride toward Pir Gourèye. It is a rebel village, a refuge for disloyal subjects of the king. Adanson, you should never choose our route simply because it seems the easiest way! The most successful traps are those into which we cheerfully throw ourselves simply because we have abandoned our fate to the comfort of the path before us. Moreover, in the bush, predators are—"

Already wearying of the string of proverbs that Ndiak was threatening to reel off, index finger raised, I interrupted him to ask what his point was. He explained to me then, in a few brief phrases, that the village of Pir Gourèye was ruled by a great marabout who reproached the king for not strictly obeying the rules of Islam. The king drank alcohol, did not respect the five daily prayers, had married many more than his allotted four wives, and lapsed into witchcraft and

worshipping the occult powers of the bush. Worst of all for
the most recent kings of Kayor, who had preceded the reign of
Mam Bathio Samb, was that their free subjects—when they
feared being reduced to slavery by Kayor's warriors, who were
as pagan as their master—ran to take refuge in Pir Gourèye.
There, they became *talibés*, disciples of the great marabout.
And in exchange for his protection and his teaching them the
true precepts of Islam, the refugees cultivated his fields. Even
though this holy man had practically no army to speak of, he
inspired enough fear that the king of Kayor did not dare attack his village. Since his policies were supposedly Moham-
medan, the king had no choice but to keep a cool head and
act like a man who has stepped on a thorn from a *sump*—the
Wolof word for a desert date palm—but who strives to walk
without limping, out of pride before his "equals."

"The best course of action," Ndiak added, proud of com-
paring the king of Kayor to a lame man, "is to avoid going
to Pir Gourèye, where we are unlikely to receive a warm welcome given where we have just come from. Instead, we should
go west to the village of Sassing, from where we can reach
Keur Damel before turning southward to Ben in Cap Vert,
our final destination. We must create our own itinerary. In
the words of a proverb which I am inventing as I speak—if
you please, Adanson!—A good man finds no honor in following a well-trodden path, but in clearing a new path—oh yes."

Ndiak did not sense the irony in my voice when I asked
him where he had acquired his wisdom. Index finger pointing
at my chest, he replied that intelligence was ageless.

Despite his immodesty, his advice was not necessarily
wrong. His explanation about the king of Kayor's difficult

relations with the great marabout of Pir Gourèye would find its place in the memorandum I wrote for Estoupan de la Brüe. There was no sense in offending the king of Kayor by pointing out, to use Ndiak's metaphor, the thorn in his foot.

Seized by the desire to have the last word and to prove to him that I too could speak in proverbs if I wished, after a few seconds of reflection I told him that I would follow his advice, "because the most powerful kings can become vicious if you are impudent enough to show that you do not believe them to be as tough as they wish to appear."

Ndiak smiled, then told me I was both right and wrong. I was right to follow his advice and wrong to wish to speak in proverbs, as he did, because my Wolof was not fluent enough to prevent me from making crude remarks when I intended to express the loftiest ideas. When I had used the word "powerful" in reference to kings, I had meant their omnipotence, the limitless power that they generally wished to exercise over their subjects, but what I had actually evoked was their sexual potency. I had mixed up two different words. And Ndiak, explaining this mistake as we rode side by side, blinked with his usual fury while trying not to laugh. He was trying not to hurt my pride. After all, even though I was white and a commoner, he had ended up convincing himself that I was his "equal."

Indeed, the day before we left Meckhé, I gave him a glimpse of my family tree, and I think I managed to convince him that my surname could be traced back to a distant Scottish ancestor who had gone to Auvergne, and whose descendants had spread all over Provence. Always very keen on family origins, Ndiak first asked me who the Scots were.

When I told him that they were a warlike people who had always fought against their neighbors, the English, and that consequently it was natural that a Scottish Adanson should have taken refuge in Auvergne under the protection of the king of France, I could tell he started to look at me in a different way.

His vision of the world had, to some extent, rubbed off on mine. It was while presenting my family history in a way that emphasized its warrior origins that I realized to what extent the opinion we have of ourselves depends on where we are and to whom we are talking. As I told Ndiak about my genealogy, I understood that when you learn a foreign language, you simultaneously absorb another conception of life, which is every bit the equal of your own.

So I followed Ndiak's advice and we immediately left the road to Pir Gourèye and headed west. We passed through several hamlets, all of which quickly emptied at our approach, and after a three-day walk from Meckhé we arrived at the village of Keur Damel. Located less than a quarter of a league from the Atlantic shore, Keur Damel—which means "the king's house" in Wolof—was a village that appeared or disappeared depending on the movements of the king of Kayor and his inner circle. The king went there to negotiate directly with European merchants. It was there, no doubt, that he had bought Ndiak's English saddle, perhaps in return for a certain number of slaves. Seeing that place, where only a few thatched fences, blown to the ground by the ocean wind, gave any hint of its occasional human population, I shivered.

The air that swept through the ghost village was not particularly cool, but I felt cold, perhaps due to the contrast with the torrid heat we had suffered on our journey up to that moment. I felt a sudden weariness as a fever took hold of me. My throat had been sore that morning, and now it suddenly became inflamed, as if someone had set fire to dry kindling. I looked at Ndiak, who sat on his horse beside me, and I think I remember asking him, in my rusty voice, a question that had been on my mind since we had been in that spot, staring at the fences half-buried in the sand of Keur Damel. How many lineages of men and women had vanished into the horizon of the ocean, so close to the village? Even now I cannot be sure that I really posed that question. If I did, I have forgotten his answer. Before collapsing from my horse, I saw his frightened face and felt his right hand grip my shoulder as he tried to stop me falling.

XIX

I woke in the middle of the night, in an indeterminate place, the strangeness of which led me to think that it was the fruit of a delirium caused by my fever. I knew that I was lying inside a hut because of the peculiar smell that they all have: the floral scent of the straw roof; earth and dried cow dung from the walls; acrid smoke from the hearth. My eyes opened to a darkness that was, in fact, something else. A cloud of bluish light, translucent, almost imperceptible, seemed to be floating above me. I imagined myself in an intermediate space between the immensity of the universe and our Earth, a place on the border where the ethereal night of our galaxy is illuminated by the last vapors of our planet's atmosphere. Had this been the glimmer of dawn, the light ought to have come in through a few cracks in the hut's roof or its door, but, there, the blue light remained equal to itself, unreal, suspended in the upper reaches of the hut and too dim to illuminate its contents. I was lying there motionless, blinking as I tried to measure the degree of intensity of this obscure light, when I was struck by a particular smell, added to the ones I already recognized.

It was the smell of saltwater mixed with fresh seaweed. A

pleasant smell, and its cool salt tang freed me from the anxiety I had been feeling at finding myself in a place where darkness was not darkness. I thought I could make out the sound of lapping water, but I could not be certain that I wasn't hearing things. Reassured by the thought that at least one of my senses was not in the grip of a hallucination, and that this meant I was still alive, I closed my eyes and fell asleep.

When I woke again, daylight had made its way into the hut. I could see the inner face of the roof, which was cluttered with a forest of yellow-bellied calabashes of all sizes, hanging there, although I could not see how. I was lying on a mat just above the ground, flat on my back, bare-chested, my body covered from feet to chin by a heavy cotton pagne which did not keep me warm. Another pagne, rolled up, lay beneath my neck. Although I was very weak, as though I had not eaten for a long time, I felt good. I wasn't thirsty, and my fever had gone. That euphoria which convalescents feel as soon as their bodies are no longer suffering began to softly fill me, relaxing my arms and legs, which I stretched. Suddenly, the large woven rush mat that sealed the raised entrance to the hut was lifted up, admitting a flood of blinding light. I immediately closed my eyes. When I opened them again, a shadow stood facing me.

But before I continue telling you what happened in that hut, my dear Aglaé—an event that marked me for life—it is necessary that I retrace my steps a little so that you can better imagine the details of the extraordinary situation in which I found myself. What I am about to tell you—and which seems to me essential to understanding what comes next in my narrative—I found out only three days after my fall from the horse. I heard it straight from Ndiak's mouth, following a barely conceivable ordeal.

When we saw each other again, Ndiak told me that, when he tried to stop me falling off that horse with no name in Keur Damel, he had initially thought that I had been struck dead, as had happened to one of his young uncles on the way back from a hunting expedition. According to Ndiak, his uncle had been punished by a bush genie because he had not correctly followed the rituals meant to appease the game he had killed. And while he had for a time believed that the occult forces of the bush had no power over me because I was white, as soon as he saw me slipping from my saddle, Ndiak had remembered my crime. The day before, on the road to Keur Damel, on the outskirts of the village of Djoff, I had shot a sacred bird, which had been perched on the branch of a mango tree. Some villagers who had heard my gunshot would have killed me in retaliation had not our little armed troop held them at bay.

Convinced that the sacred bird's spirit had avenged itself on me, which proved that I had lost some aspect of my whiteness by learning to speak Wolof, Ndiak had laid my body on the sand of Keur Damel. For him, I was already dead. To make sure, he had searched for a pulse at my jugular and my wrist and had felt nothing. He was just starting to wonder whether he should bury me where I lay, and in accordance with which religious ritual, when the oldest warrior of our escort had taken a small mirror from one of his pockets. This man, who was about fifty—quite an advanced age for a warrior in

Senegal—was named Seydou Gadio. Until then, I had paid no particular attention to him. He was very discreet, and only his white hair made him stand out. And yet it was he who led our voyage. He saved my life on this occasion, though only to reduce me to wretchedness again less than a week later.

Seydou Gadio knelt next to my head and placed the mirror just in front of my nose and mouth. The surface of the glass misted over, proof that I was still breathing. Seydou Gadio was a man of great experience, and Ndiak had no qualms in admitting, when he told me what had happened during the two days when I was unconscious, that he had relied completely on the old soldier. It was, then, Seydou Gadio who had ordered the construction of a stretcher from the remnants of a fence buried in the sand at the village of Keur Damel. And he it was who had commanded the men of the troop he was leading to take turns carrying me, at top speed, to the village of Ben in Cap Vert.

Both Seydou Gadio and Ndiak himself had thought it preferable to have me taken to Ben as quickly as possible. The lethargy into which I had been plunged by a high fever was, they believed, a blessing, smoothing out the difficulties of a journey that a vivid awareness of my own suffering would have rendered more complicated. Had they stopped frequently and traveled slowly to spare me, I would have lost the last of my strength needed to fight off the evil that had already won the first battle against my body. If that evil believed me already defeated, since my breathing was imperceptible, it would not bother attacking me again. The cooler climate of Cap Vert would help my rehabilitation, to the great surprise—so they believed—of the spirit I had offended by killing the sacred bird in the village of Djoff.

Ndiak and Seydou thought it best to conceal me from the spirit's sight. To hide me, they covered my whole body with a cotton sheet, white like a shroud. Every time the stretcher-bearers stopped to take a rest, they would surreptitiously lift up the edges of the sheet to moisten my burning face with cool water. Having done that, they would cover my face again and shake their heads, as if lamenting my death. Ndiak told me that he would often sigh softly, but loud enough to be heard by the genie of the sacred bird: "May God forgive him. It was written in the heavens that he had to depart without being able to bid farewell to his loved ones in France."

Thus it was that my stretcher was carried at great speed to Cap Vert, avoiding villages as much as possible. After fording a creek that flowed into a saltwater lake where the water turned bright pink when the sun was at its zenith—as I had seen for myself during my previous trip to Cap Vert—they chose to walk under the cover of the Krampsanè Forest in order to throw pursuing death off my trail. They did this at great risk to their own lives, because that great forest of palm trees and date palms is also home to lions, panthers, and hyenas who emerge at night to prowl the outskirts of the villages of Cap Vert by the sea.

After a thirty-hour forced march, they arrived at the village of Ben. There was a full moon that night, and, on the edge of the village, Ndiak and Seydou Gadio spotted the silhouettes of a hyena and a lion, side by side, their forepaws resting on the roof of the hut in which I would eventually awake, devouring fish that had been hung there to dry. Seydou, the old warrior, signaled for the troop to stop. And they waited there until the two wild animals, who were clearly friends even though lions and hyenas are believed to be mortal enemies, returned to the forest at dawn, paying no attention to their human observers.

Ndiak told me that the chief of the village of Ben had not been fazed by the account of the lion and the hyena working together to steal the dried fish. He had simply replied: "Everybody has to live." He also showed no surprise at seeing me transported on a stretcher: "Our healer already told me that strangers would ask to see her today. Follow me, I will lead you to her."

Ndiak related their surprise at being led back the way they had come, to an enclosure on the edge of the village, to the very hut on whose roof they had seen the dried fish being taken by the lion and the hyena just an hour before. To Ndiak and Seydou, this had seemed like an omen, although neither of them could say whether it was good or evil.

As they had expected—because the power to heal is generally associated in men's minds with a long experience of life—they were welcomed at the enclosure's entrance by an old woman who, before they could explain the situation, told them she would heal the white man lying on a stretcher even though she hated all those of his race. My two companions shuddered at this because they had not yet lifted up the shroud that covered every part of me. How had she known I was a *toubab*? They were no more reassured by what the woman said next: she had known for a long time who we were and that we would come to meet her.

Ndiak admitted that both he and Seydou Gadio, despite

the warrior's age and experience, were intimidated by this healing woman. She leaned on a long staff covered with red leather embedded with cowries, and her face was half-hidden by a sort of hood made from the skin of a gigantic snake. The snakeskin also covered her shoulders and fell all the way down to her feet, like a living coat. Jet-black, with pale yellow stripes, the skin had a gleaming, oily sheen. Ndiak had the impression that the old woman, when she turned around and limped back toward the main hut in her enclosure— where she had ordered me to be taken—was not merely an old woman but some kind of indefinable being, half-human, half-snake. Beneath that hideous coat, the healer's entire body was hidden inside a close-fitting clay-red garment. And the lower half of her face, the only visible part of her, was smeared with an amalgam of whitish dried earth, with cracks at the corners of her lips that made her mouth look as wide as the vile snake jaws that swallowed up the top of her head. Despite her advanced age, betrayed by her bent back, her movements were quick and agile and she punctuated every word she spoke, in a deep, solemn voice, by slamming the base of her long staff against the ground. It was thus that she ordered Ndiak, Seydou Gadio, and the rest of our troop not to camp near her enclosure. They were to stay at the other end of the village and she would summon them once I had been healed.

My companions obeyed her, believing that my fate was no longer in their hands but in the hands of this healer, whose appearance was so frightening that they imagined she would defeat the evil spirit who tormented me—that of the sacred bird I had shot with a musket in the village of Djoff. Ndiak admitted to me that he had, despite everything, prayed to

God many times that I would escape death, because he knew that if I died he would have to tell his father the real reason for our voyage to Ben. He was afraid the king would lose respect for me if he learned that we had made that long journey from the island of Saint-Louis out of simple curiosity to hear the far-fetched tale of a slave who had supposedly returned from America. He thought my discredit would rebound onto him, leading his "equals" to mock him.

"Of course, Adanson," he concluded, after describing our extraordinary arrival at the healing woman's hut in Ben, "I would also have mourned your death as a friend. But the hardest thing for me would have been admitting to others that I had aided a madman."

With these words, spoken in a voice of absolute seriousness by Ndiak in the shade of an ebony tree, I thought I understood that my young friend was already scheming to become king of Waalo. Hearing him speak thus, it occurred to me that he would have no qualms about fomenting a war to overturn the line of succession, according to which one of his nephews would inherit the throne. Perhaps he was already seeking to clothe himself in a mantle of respectability, of which I was one of the key elements simply because I was white. I began to reconsider the trust I had put in him, because a man who sets forth on the path that leads to power, however young he might be, sees those closest to him merely as pawns to be moved at will across a vast chessboard.

But I was wrong. Ndiak was, I think, the most faithful friend I ever had.

X X

When I awoke, after two days of utter lethargy, a shadow stood in front of me. And when I saw, in the hut's half light, after my eyes had adjusted to the dazzle, the lower half of that hideous face, I thought I would faint again. Standing at the foot of my bed, a human being observed me silently, and, in the space of a second of terror, I thought an immense boa was readying itself to attack me, its mouth wide open. I sat up abruptly on my elbows and asked in a weak voice what the monster wanted of me. I received no response. It observed me, its eyes concealed under a snakeskin hood that emitted a stench of rancid butter mixed with the telling odor of burned eucalyptus bark. It was then that I realized I must be in the company of one of those healers initiated into the mysteries of the plants of their land, whose knowledge I had sought out as soon as I had learned enough Wolof to understand them. If I was conscious again, it was undoubtedly thanks to this person, and I had nothing to fear from her.

She stood motionless, staring at me with invisible eyes for a period of time that seemed very long to me. Then, as if making a sudden and irrevocable decision, she took hold of her hood in both hands and threw it back over her shoulders.

"And you—what do you want of Maram Seck?"

I thought I was hallucinating again: the woman I saw before me was young and, it struck me, very beautiful despite the plastering of white earth that defaced her cheeks and mouth. Untouched by this white mask, the top half of her face revealed the profound blackness of her skin, the very fine and lustrous texture of which suggested softness. Her braided hair gathered in a high bun, and her long and slender neck, gave her the bearing of a queen of the Ancient World. The almond shape of her eyes, accentuated by their long, curved lashes, reminded me of an Egyptian bust I had once seen in the cabinet of curiosities belonging to my old botany teacher, Bernard de Jussieu. Her irises, as deeply black as her skin, clashed with the snowy whiteness of her pupils, and these extraordinary eyes were trained on me as though I were the woman's prey. They stared, still and unblinking as a hypnotist's. I was intimidated and, while I hesitated to answer her question, she bent down to pick up from the floor, without taking her eyes off me, a machete, which she brought close to my head.

"If you don't tell me who you are and why you have come here with your escort, I will cut your throat. I have no fear of death."

"My name is Michel Adanson," I replied instantly, "and since you have introduced yourself as Maram Seck, I will admit to you frankly that I came to meet you out of curiosity. I have come in the company of Ndiak, the son of the king of Waalo, to hear your story from your own lips."

"So you're the one he sent to flush me out, like a hunted animal!"

"Who is *he*?"

"Baba Seck, my uncle, chief of the village of Sor."

"Is it not natural that he should be concerned about your fate?"

"He is concerned less for me than for himself."

"What do you mean?"

Realizing that my incomprehension was genuine, Maram Seck put down the machete with which she had been threatening me and went on: "Baba Seck is a wretch. It is because of him that I must hide myself far from Sor in the guise of an old healer …"

She fell silent, probably because she had spoken these last words in a shaky voice and she was one of those people who are too proud to weep in front of others. And perhaps also because she needed to know my precise connection to Baba Seck.

Sensing that I had to reassure her before she would begin to tell me her story, I explained what her uncle had told me about her disappearance from Sor, the steps he had taken in the bush and on the island of Saint-Louis to find her, the messengers he had sent to the neighboring villages to ask whether her abductors had been seen, because no one in Sor doubted that she had been kidnapped by strangers and sold to slave traders. I added that Baba Seck, on the night when he told me about her, had said that a few days before that, a man named Senghane Faye had traveled to the village of Ben to announce her presence there, after returning alive from the Americas, but had forbidden anyone from Sor to try to find her again.

When I finished by explaining that her uncle's story had intrigued me so much that I had decided to walk from the island of Saint-Louis to the village of Ben in Cap Vert to find out for myself, she seemed to relax. And, to spare me the uncomfortable position in which I found myself—because I was still lying down, propped up on my elbows—she picked up a carved wooden stool and drew it close to the bed so she could sit next to me. That meant I could continue to look at her while resting my head on the rolled-up cloth that served as my pillow. She lowered her eyes toward me from time to time, so close that I could smell her floral scent beneath the sour smell of shea butter and burned eucalyptus that came from the snakeskin she wore.

As a silence grew between us and we no longer dared look at each other for longer than an instant, Maram Seck suddenly asked me if it was possible that a white man, from the race of the masters of the sea, should make such a long journey by foot out of simple curiosity about her. I replied that I was there not only for her, but to discover new plants and observe the animals of the bush between the island of Saint-Louis and Cap Vert. My work was to tally up the plants, trees, shells, and animals—of both land and sea—in order to describe them in great detail in books so that other men and women in France could learn from a distance about what I had seen in Senegal. So if she had not existed, my journey would not have been wasted, because I would have increased my knowledge of the plants, trees, and animals of her country.

"So you are different from those people at the Senegal Concession," Maram Seck asked me, "who trade in ivory, gold, gum arabic, leather, and slaves?"

Very happy to present myself as an exceptional man, I replied that I had nothing to do with the people at the Senegal

Concession and that any association I might have with them was purely a matter of form. I was in Senegal only to observe its fauna and flora.

"But surely you know," she retorted, "that the Senegal Concession will seek to profit from your observations? Either you are naïve or you are a hypocrite."

Those words frightened me even more than her machete. I was starting to feel concerned by her opinion of me. So I launched into a long explanation about the particular nature of my work in Senegal, although I did so hesitantly because I did not wish to appear immodest. Thinking oneself different from others betrays a desire for distinction, and I felt in a confused way that if I wished to prove myself worthy of the nobility of soul that I sensed in this young woman, and perhaps win her affection, I would have to be careful what I said. This was all the more difficult, since I was speaking Wolof—a language whose every nuance I fervently wished I could master at that very moment, so as to present myself in the best possible light—and since my brain was still fogged by the after-effects of my fever.

Maram Seck let me lose myself in these confused explanations for a while, in which I feigned modesty while boasting of how different I was from all the other Frenchmen in Senegal, until—perhaps noticing that I was starting to look tired and drawn—she abruptly stood up, unceremoniously interrupting my little speech, every word of which was underpinned by the nascent love she inspired in me.

She went over to a dark corner of the hut, of which I could make out nothing from where I lay, and came back almost immediately to sit next to me, holding a little calabash in the shape of a bowl with a curved handle. She handed it to me and I slowly drank its contents, a mix of curdled cow's milk and powder from the fruit of a baobab tree, known as monkey bread, the acid taste of which quenched my thirst better than water would have done, and which filled me up as if I were eating bread. It must also have been an effective medicine, because I felt my strength return more quickly than I would have thought possible. Then, after covering her shoulders and head again with the hood of her black and yellow striped snakeskin, hiding the upper half of her face, she helped me to my feet and supported me as I walked outside the hut.

It was September, close to the end of the rainy season. The sky was full of thick clouds, the color of a young eggplant, which were gradually darkening—as though the wind that carried them through the sky had forced them to swallow all the red dust from the earth of Cap Vert, to be returned later in a downpour.

Maram Seck guided me to a corner of the courtyard surrounded by a fence the height of a man. There I saw a large brown earthenware jar with a weathered finish and a flared neck, in which a wooden bowl was floating. She indicated that I could use this to wash myself. A small black bar of soap, made from a mix of ash and a hardened paste that smelled of eucalyptus leaves, was resting on a wisp of soft straw the size of the palm of my hand. Maram helped me take off my shirt, which she held at arm's length and tossed into a nearby calabash filled with water. She would give me clean, dry clothes when I returned to the hut, where she would wait for me.

The sky was threatening to crack open, and since I knew, having read it before my voyage to Senegal, that rainwater was full of germs, I did not dally. I washed myself thoroughly, then did the same to my shirt, my breeches, and my stockings. Seeing the water in the calabash where I had rubbed my clothing with soap turn the same eggplant color as the stormy sky above us, I understood Maram's disgust and felt ashamed of myself. Once I was clean, and once my clothes appeared to be approaching their original color after five successive washes, I hung them over the top of the fence that protected this place from indiscreet eyes. The wind was rising. I just had time to cover myself with a pagne that Maram had left me before running to the hut, where she was waiting for me. The woven rush mat that sealed the entrance was lifted. Safely sheltered, I turned around to watch the tornado.

First I saw sheets of bloodred water come pouring from the sky. It was this first rain that was dangerous for one's health. Once this impure torrent was over, the water that fell to earth was clean and drinkable. So it is that, in the villages of Senegal, the lids are removed from all the rainwater jars soon after the beginning of a storm.

When I returned to the hut, Maram was preparing to go out, her head uncovered, wearing only a pagne, the top of the cloth running under her armpits. Outside, she ran from jar to jar, from water pot to water pot, removing all the lids. I saw her disappear behind one of the huts in the enclosure, presumably to remove the lids of all the other receptacles. At first I was surprised to see her go out without her usual disguise. Then I supposed that she had no fear of being caught unawares by the villagers just then, in the middle of a storm, because they were all busy doing the same thing: collecting water from the sky.

I left the entrance to the hut open and went back to my bed, where Maram had stripped off the bedclothes and pagnes soiled by my sweat and replaced them with clean ones. Incense smoke was rising through the holes—in the shapes of triangles, squares, and half moons—in a small ocher earthenware pot, perfuming the air with the heavy, intoxicating smell of musk, mixed with eucalyptus bark. Just then I noticed a large wooden tub, circled with a strip of metal, on the floor to the right of the hut's entrance. When I thought I heard, coming from this tub, the same lapping sound that had brought me back to consciousness the previous night, I went over to take a closer look. After removing its lid, a sort of wide fan made of woven rushes, I dipped my index finger in the water and hastily took it out again when I saw the surface of the liquid move. I licked my finger: it tasted salty. I realized that the tub must be home to one or two fish from the sea, whose movements had made the lapping sound. I was surprised by this, until it occurred to me that Maram could be breeding them for use in her healing practices.

I returned to my bed, where I found a pair of white cotton trousers and a long shirt with open sides that Maram had left there for me. The shirt was made of indienne, and I was struck by its charming printed patterns. Decorated with purple crabs and yellow and blue fish, it was also scattered with pink shells, each one hidden in a bouquet of pale green seaweed, against a perfectly white background. I was touched by Maram's thoughtfulness: she had given me clothes that were visibly new, and I wished I could shave so that she would see me at my best. Touching a hand to my cheeks, I felt a three-day beard whose red color, the same hue as my hair, surely didn't flatter me. But my toiletries were not to hand. Maram had explained to me that the trunks containing my belongings were at the other end of the village, in the care of Ndiak. I could not go and fetch them, though, nor let my traveling companions know that I was feeling better, because the rain was still hammering down. I decided to go back to bed so that I could continue to gather my strength while I awaited Maram's return.

I was on the verge of falling asleep, thinking how eager I was for her to come back so that I could hear the rest of her story, when I heard to my left, behind the wall against which the bed was leaning, the scraping noise of a lid being removed from a jar—presumably Maram continuing to collect rainwater. Curious to see her, I stood up on my bed and, on tiptoes, was able to peer through the gap between the lower part of the thatched roof and the top of the hut's wall. What I saw through that crack made me shiver.

I had almost entered the priesthood in my early youth, a few years before my voyage to Senegal, and as a fervent Catholic I attached to modesty the great virtue of preventing us from too often committing the sins of the flesh. Despite the principles of my religious education, and despite my desire to tear myself away from that horribly dangerous and beautiful sight, I could not take my eyes off Maram Seck: completely naked, she was busy lifting the lids from all the receptacles that she hoped the storm would fill with water. She had taken off her pagne, I supposed, because the drenched cloth was inhibiting her movements, and now she was running around as lovely and free in her total nudity as a Black Eve not yet exiled from paradise. The rain had washed the white earthen mask from her face, revealing high cheekbones and dimples that could just be discerned on her cheeks even when she was not smiling. Her breasts, swollen with life, looked like they had been polished by a sculptor, and the slenderness of her waist accentuated the splendid roundness of her lower back and her upper thighs. Unaware that I was spying upon her, she was completely uninhibited in her movements, and not an inch of her anatomy escaped my gaze, allowing me to reach the conclusion that, even though she was a grown woman, not a single part of her body bore any trace of hair.

The spectacle that she unwittingly offered me was probably over very quickly, because she soon went to another part of the enclosure. But in the few seconds that it lasted, I reproached myself a hundred times for lacking the willpower to tear my eyes away from the myriad beauties of Maram Seck. And I went back to bed in that state, sick with desire and with shame at having abused with my eyes and my thoughts this young woman who had no idea I was spying on her nakedness in that providential downpour.

XXI

Maram did not return to the hut until the rain had ceased. She had put on a white cotton gown and she smelled of freshly cut grass. I didn't dare say a word, so ashamed did I feel at having seen her naked, promising myself that I would beg her forgiveness on a false pretext so that she would grant it to me without knowing the real reason.

Now that I am an old man, I do not believe that the sin for which I reproached myself was really so great. Is it not absurd to attach moral judgments to natural urges? But I must acknowledge that it was my religion that kept me from offending Maram Seck. Had I made advances, I would almost certainly have lost her trust and she would not have told me her story. If the world in which we lived had given us that chance, I would have one day asked her to marry me. And if she had accepted, I would have known her, in the way nature invites us to when a man loves a woman and a woman loves a man.

Maram and I sat cross-legged facing each other on the bed from which I had spied upon her less than an hour before. She was very close to me; I could have touched her by reaching out my hand. Her big eyes stared into mine, and they were filled with a candor that made my heart ache. How I wanted to hold her in my arms! All her movements were gentle and agile, with a graceful charm that fascinated me. The hut was still filled with daylight and I noticed that the palms of her hands, which she waved slightly when she grew animated, were decorated with geometric designs. Circles, triangles . . . dark ocher-colored dots had been imprinted on her skin using dye made from henna, a plant I had described in one of my memoranda. I had the impression that those signs told her story in a secret script that she alone could decipher, like those fortune-telling Gypsies who can read the course of entire lives in their victims' palms.

"I have decided to reveal to you my true self, not to hide anything from you," Maram went on in a soft voice, "because I believe I can trust you. You seem different from other men, those of my own race as well as yours."

Her first words made me blush. She didn't know how wrong she was.

"A woman's beauty can be a curse," she said. "I was barely out of childhood when it brought me all the misfortune that led me here, to this hut in the village of Ben.

"One day, I do not remember when exactly, my uncle—my mother's older brother, who had acted as my father since my parents' death—no longer saw me as a child. Little by little, it seemed to me that he would look only at me, surrounded as I was by his own children, when we came to his hut to greet him every morning. To start with, I was proud of the attention he showed me and I strove to deserve it by being as gracious as possible. I thought I was lucky to have been welcomed into his home. But soon I felt puzzled by the way he looked at me. He would follow me everywhere I went inside the enclosure, so insistently that I had the unpleasant feeling that he was pulling my hair, grabbing my shoulders, tearing my clothes, devouring me. I tried as hard as I could to remove myself from his sight. In vain. I felt like a gazelle that, despite its incredible leaps, its ability to sprint in one direction and then another, cannot shake off the predator shadowing its every move.

"I quickly realized that I was at my uncle's mercy, the prisoner of a man's desire when I was still only a child. Exhausted by the continual threat of a disaster I did not deserve, I decided to concentrate on keeping as much distance between us as possible. So it was that I would often escape my uncle's enclosure, and even the village itself, so as not to be alone in his presence. Soon I was spending most of my days in the bush around Sor.

"My uncle Baba Seck and his wife tolerated my escapades for different reasons. She, because she must have sensed I was becoming her rival, because I threatened her despite my innocence. He, because he planned no doubt to abuse me in some dark part of the bush, away from prying eyes. My younger cousins were surprised and resentful of the freedom I had to go beyond the borders of our village and to be exempt from the household chores that they were forced to perform. Soon, the only domestic work for which I was solely responsible was bringing back, before nightfall, some dry kindling to light the hearth for our evening meal.

"At first, I was as frightened of the bush as I was of my uncle, but in the end it became my refuge, my family. Through my explorations and observations, through watching the animals that populated the bush until I became one of them myself, I learned the virtues of many plants. Most of the knowledge that serves me now in my role as healer, here in the village of Ben, I owe to those three years when I would not return to my uncle's enclosure until dusk, my arms always full of kindling for the kitchen fire.

"The villagers in Sor thought my way of life strange, to begin with. Then they became used to it. All the men and women I passed in the mornings, on the way to their *lougan*, their field, just outside the village, would greet me cordially. I was still only a child, but many of them started to ask me to bring them herbs or flowers, whose virtues for healing this or that illness they would briefly explain to me. Either they had noticed these virtues themselves, or their parents had taught them. And soon, after gathering all this scattered knowledge which they willingly gave me, I knew more than anyone else in the village.

"I gained a degree of fame when I managed to heal one of my cousins who, despite continuing to have a healthy appetite, was visibly wasting away. It was said in the village that she was being eaten from within by a witch, by a *dëmm* who wished harm on her family. I think at least some people believed that *I* might have been that malevolent witch. I decided to heal Sagar so that this rumor, which had begun to reach me, would not spread any further.

"I owed my success to the good fortune of being able to observe animals in the bush behaving in a natural way. They had become accustomed to my discreet presence. I had silently entered their world.

"One day, I saw a small green monkey, separated from its clan, that was so skinny I thought it must be ill, stuffing its mouth with roots from a shrub that it had patiently dug up, then chewing them for a long time. Intrigued, I followed it at a distance and, a little later, observed it relieving itself with little yelps of pain and then of satisfaction after it turned around to see what it had expelled. On the ground, writhing in the monkey's excrement, was a very long worm, surrounded by dozens of smaller worms. I was able to examine them more closely once the monkey had moved away. I concluded from this that what had cured that animal could do the same for humans afflicted with the same condition. So it was that, imagining that my cousin Sagar had worms in her gut, since she was losing weight despite all she ate, I prepared a decoction of that root and told her to drink it. Soon she was rid of those parasites that had been reaping all the benefit of the food she consumed.

"It was from this feat that my reputation as a healer stemmed, and my uncle, as chief of the village, trumpeted the news that we would no longer have to go elsewhere to heal our sick. It was true that the healer in a village quite a distance from ours demanded too many payments in kind for his work. For myself, happy that I was able to heal almost everyone who came to me, I received only those gifts that were offered freely.

"My uncle Baba Seck rejoiced at seeing his favored treatment of me justified, having let me wander through the bush around Sor while the other children were forbidden to leave the village. I gave him everything I received as payment from my patients: chickens, eggs, millet, sometimes even sheep. He could have continued to profit from the wealth I was bringing him with my knowledge and to consolidate his position as chief of the village through my reputation, but he was incapable of taming the demon that possessed him: he wanted my body, even though I was his niece, a child who had grown up among his own children.

"It was true that during those three years of half freedom, I had grown so much that my budding womanhood, first detected by my uncle, was now in full bloom. Whenever I saw him he would stare at me fiercely and insistently, with unconcealed desire, but I thought I could also see in his eyes a deep distress, the remorse of a man constantly battling with himself, with no respite, with no hope of ever healing the disease of his love for me.

"The pity I felt for my uncle must have aroused the anger of my *faru rab*, my husband-genie, who apparently decided that I must leave my native village before the earth of Sor was sullied by a crime of incest. Perhaps too my frequent visits to the bush had excited the jealousy of a female genie whose powers surpassed those of my *rab*. Whatever the reason, the bush that had until then been my refuge suddenly grew hostile toward me.

"I, who had never been caught unawares by any creature crawling, running, or flying through the bush in many years; I, who was warned in advance of the slightest danger by white-throated sparrows or crested hoopoes; I, who had learned all the tricks used by prey to escape their predators—I did not see him until he was only a few steps away from me. Too late.

"My uncle grabbed me and held me tight in his arms. He is a big, strong man and I was not able to fight him off. Wild-eyed, he whispered in my ear, as if afraid he would be overheard in that place empty of any person other than me:

'Maram, Maram, you know what I want. You've known it for a long time. Let's do it just once. Only once, I promise. No one will know. Afterward, I'll find you a good husband . . . Be kind to me, just once!'

"My uncle was right: I knew what he wanted. But I did not want it. Once I had seen, in the shade of a copse, a young villager with his wife who had come to bring him some food while he worked his field. They didn't notice me as I spied upon them, hidden behind a tree, watching their frenetic, joyous dance, sometimes him on top of her, sometimes her on top of him. They looked so happy. I heard them moan and even cry out with joy at the end.

"But I, imprisoned in my uncle's powerful arms, was moaning only with terror. It was unthinkable that I should do that thing with him. We had the same blood, the same name. If he got what he desired, we would be lost—him, me, the village of Sor and the fields surrounding it, which would go into an irrevocable decline, soiled by our impure act. It was not in the order of the world that he should treat me like his wife.

"I struggled, but my uncle managed to throw me to the ground and he lay on top of me with his full weight. He stank of burned wood and acrid sweat, and his face was twisted in a feverish, ferocious expression. Sweat was dripping from his forehead into my eyes, my mouth. I yelled at him that he ought to give me a husband, not become one. I called him Papa, to try to bring him back to himself. I tried to remind him of my mother's name, of my little sister Faty Seck, my father and his cousin Bocum Seck. I shouted out the names of his children—Galaye, Ndiogou, Sagar, and Fama Seck—to make him remember that I was one of them. But he was no longer himself. He was blinded by desire. He didn't even know who I was anymore. He wanted me, then and there, at any price. To penetrate me.

"He had already torn off the pagne that covered me and he was trying to part my thighs when the sound of laughter, bursting suddenly from the bush, not far from the copse of trees where we were, stopped him in his tracks.

"Every tongue has its own way of laughing. The one I heard then was unknown to me, and, even though it had caused my uncle to let go of me, I continued to tremble with fear. Perhaps my *rab*, my genie protector, had materialized into some sort of being, half-human and half-inhuman, to save me from the desperate situation in which I was caught. If my *rab* had dissociated itself from me to the point where it could no longer rejoin my body, I might easily lose my mind. I had been able to survive in the bush only thanks to him. I sensed his presence in my dreams, in various human or animal forms, without being able to tie him to any of them in particular, without yet—back then—being able to recognize him.

"However, he who had saved me from my uncle's monstrous desire was not an avatar of my *rab*, but a white man like you, Adanson. Flanked by two Black warriors, he walked over to us, laughing in a jerky, high-pitched way, like a young hyena. He was taller than you and he carried a musket, as did his two companions. They must have been hunting in the Sor bush, and my *rab* had guided their steps to save me from my uncle. But, as I would soon discover, he had swapped one great evil for another.

"My uncle stood up, and as I got up too, groping for my

pagne so I could cover my nakedness, the white man stopped laughing. He stood petrified as he watched me dress, all his attention focused on me, his gaze avid. He was wearing a hat with a wide brim and part of his face lay in shadow. His eyes shone. I had not seen many white men in my life: two at most, and from a distance, men who had come to the island of Saint-Louis to hunt in the bush around our village. This one was different, terrifying. The skin of his face was covered with innumerable little holes and marks, like those that you can see on the face of the full moon when it rises from the horizon, at the threshold of the sky. The wings of his nose were swollen, crisscrossed with little purplish fissures, and between his thick lips I could see his black-flecked teeth.

"Without taking his eyes off me, he began talking in your language, in that way you have of not needing to open your mouth very wide to speak. Like the twittering of a bird. One of his two Black companions translated his words into Wolof and I learned that, without even wanting to know who we were, where we came from, what our names were, the white man wanted to buy me as a slave from my uncle.

"Despite everything, I still felt pity for my uncle Baba Seck. He was dejected. He stood there like a shamefaced child, caught red-handed. Whereas normally he was a leader of great presence, the man I saw beside me, facing the white man and his two Black guards, was humiliated, wretched. Head lowered, he was still retying the strings of his breeches, incapable of arguing with the poor terms of sale being dictated to him. He had been seen in the worst possible situation for a father, the head of a family, the chief of a village. But, rather than choosing to die at that instant, rather than choosing an honorable exit, I saw that he had already resigned himself to continuing to live despite the poison of the crime that would now flow eternally through his veins. My pity soon dried up when I realized that he was going to sacrifice me to preserve his little life as a chief. In fact, he looked almost relieved that fate had offered him a chance to rid himself of his niece, his temptation, his shame."

Maram had stopped speaking and was observing me as if trying to gauge the effect of her words on me. I doubt she had any difficulty perceiving my extreme emotion. I had thought I knew her uncle Baba Seck, and now I discovered that he was a very different man from the one I had imagined. Having met him so often, I would never have guessed that he could have been the cause of his niece's disappearance. He continued to live and smile, as if nothing were wrong, protected by a superficial respectability that might easily collapse in seconds were his crime to come to light. Had he managed to dissociate himself from his past and, like many humans, to build a wall between two distinct parts of his soul, one luminous and the other dark? Did he feel remorse or had he succeeded in finding a way to break free from the act that had led to the loss of Maram?

I imagined that Baba Seck had told the invented story of his niece's disappearance with a particular purpose in mind. Perhaps he had intended to pique my curiosity in order to send me out as a scout, to flush Maram out of hiding, to help him—in some way that I did not yet understand—to rid himself of her. He must have trembled at the words of Senghane

Faye, Maram's envoy, asking if her funeral had already taken place in Sor and demanding that nobody come to see her at the village of Ben. Wasn't this a way of secretly threatening to denounce him for his crime? Maram must have instructed the messenger to say all that to torture her uncle, who thought he had rid himself of her forever when he sold her to a white man.

Something else troubled me, something that would certainly complicate the plan of vengeance that she had probably dreamed up against Baba Seck. From her description of the white man with the syphilitic face, I had no doubt of his identity: it was Estoupan de la Brüe, director of the Senegal Concession. Which meant that my presence in her company was exposing Maram to danger on a scale that she could not even imagine.

XXII

While I considered what I had just been told, Maram caught her breath. Night had suddenly engulfed the big hut. In Senegal, dusk as we know it in Europe does not exist: the passage from day to night is not slow, as it is in our latitudes, but abrupt. Maram made no motion to light a lamp, and I decided she was right. What she had to tell me, as the beginning of her story had signaled, could be revealed only under cover of darkness and not in the sort of light that would have rendered the terrible spectacle of her life's wounds even more unbearable.

"My uncle Baba Seck sold me to a white man in exchange for a musket. I had to disappear if he was to be sure of going on with his former life. Even though I threw myself at his feet and begged him not to sell me, promising that I would not say anything to anyone in the village, he turned away from me with an expression of horror, as if I had become repellent to him. I forced myself not to cry out that he was my uncle in front of the two Black guards who were accompanying my white buyer and who could have translated my words. I did not want it said that Baba Seck had tried to rape his own niece. That would have poured shame on top of shame.

"My uncle, in a rush to sell me to a white man before the full extent of his crime could be revealed, took the musket held out by one of the guards and ran away without a backward glance. But I had more honor than he did. Never would the white man or his two acolytes know that I had been sold for a simple musket by my mother's own brother. That was the only thing that mattered to me then in the chaos, the catastrophe into which my uncle had delivered me. Around and inside me, the world was collapsing, but I saved my family's honor.

"My abductors wished to leave the forest around Sor as discreetly as possible. This meant they had to take me to the river—where a dugout canoe was awaiting us, moored to the roots of a mangrove tree—even though it involved a long detour. During our walk under the canopy of the forest, I could have tried to escape, to scream, to beg my *rab* and all the genies of the bush to come and help me regain my freedom, to promise myself in marriage to one of them even if it caused me to become sterile and unable to have a human family. But none of those things happened: I had neither the strength nor the will to flee. I was crushed by the misfortune that had befallen me. My legs shook; they could barely carry me. My shoulders, back, and neck all ached, and I moved forward without seeing anything around me, eyes blinded by tears, choking on sorrow and despair.

"Hidden under a fishermen's net at the bottom of the dugout, where the three men had thrown me before pushing out into the river, I quickly fell asleep despite the stagnant water that covered half of my face. And I fell into a dream in which the whole bush was dripping with blood: I spotted my *faru rab* dressed in a black and yellow pagne, waving his hand at me as if to say: 'Come back, come back!'

"He was a handsome man, tall and very strong, with gleaming skin, who wept while all around him the vegetation was red, as if the tree bark and plant stems had been splattered with the sacrifice of thousands of animals whose bodies had vanished, spirited away by djinn. My *rab* did not attempt to hide his tears from me. He yelled that he loved me and that he should have kept me for himself. He asked my forgiveness for not having protected me that day as securely as he had during the three years when we had been happy together. Then, still a prisoner of my dream, I had the impression that he was very slowly collapsing in on himself. His mouth began to widen out of all proportion; his eyes turned yellow; his head flattened and grew triangular. The pagne wrapped around him became embedded in his flesh. He coiled himself up, head raised, eyes still fixed on me. My *rab*, my protective genie, was an enormous boa. In this way, he showed himself to me in a dream long before the expected time. My initiation was not over—I was only sixteen—but this was the most important thing he could do for me before I left the bush of Sor forever.

"I woke up a different person after that fantastical dream. Having been despondent when the dugout left the shores of the forest near Sor, I now felt strangely powerful. Although my three captors trampled me underfoot, although I was struggling to breathe, trapped in the fishermen's net, and although I almost drowned in the stagnant water at the bottom of the dugout, I had the curious sensation that it was no longer myself who was in danger, but my three kidnappers. Long shivers ran down my spine in a way that was almost pleasurable, and, as night settled over the river, it seemed to me, against all evidence, that I, the prey, had become the predator.

"I felt the swaying of the dugout and imagined that my *rab*, my guardian genie, was swimming under it, waiting for the perfect moment to capsize it and rescue me. At first I thought the noises and movements I perceived under our boat were him finally attacking, but in fact it was just the hull scraping against sand as we moored on a shore of the island of Saint-Louis.

"The boat was pulled up the beach by the white man's two henchmen. They were angry with him because they had to strain and sweat to drag it far enough away from the water for him to climb out without getting his feet wet. I could hear them uttering violent curses until the white man ordered them in Wolof to shut up. They must make no noise anymore. In low voices they insulted his mother, his grandmother, and all his ancestors before roughly hauling me out of the dugout. Each of them held me under an armpit and, despite the darkness and the fishing net that covered me, I was able to see them. My senses and perceptions seemed exceptionally heightened. I thought I could see, hear, feel better than ever, as if my *faru rab*, my snake-husband, had granted me superhuman powers.

"The white man's two henchmen were warriors, mercenaries that the king of Waalo had put at his disposal to protect him on his expeditions around Saint-Louis. One of them was angrier than the other because it had been his musket that the white man had offered as payment for me. A professional warrior deprived of his weapon feels naked. Irascible and aggressive as a matter of principle, particularly after drinking the strong alcohol in which he is paid, he will kill without a second thought if he considers himself disrespected. People like that are feared and hated by all the peasants of Senegal because they are violent accomplices to the slave trade.

"I took a good look at those two mercenaries and I can tell you, Adanson, that one of the men in your escort is the same whose musket was used to buy me. He already had white hair back then. I even know his name. He is called Seydou Gadio. The other one was Ngagne Bass."

Maram fell silent, as if giving me time to absorb what she had told me. At the time, I still didn't know who this Seydou Gadio was. I would not learn that until the next day, from Ndiak. Seydou Gadio was the man who had put the little mirror in front of my mouth to check that I was still breathing when I had collapsed in Keur Damel. It was also thanks to the makeshift stretcher he had created to transport me to Ben that I was still alive. Ndiak and I had always suspected that Estoupan de la Brüe had placed one of his spies in our escort. Hearing this from Maram confirmed our suppositions in a way that was all the more ominous, since it meant yet more misfortune for her.

While I let these bitter thoughts consume me, Maram stood up in the darkness. I heard her light footsteps, then the sound of her moving the big woven rush fan that covered the top of the tub of seawater that I had discovered near the hut's entrance during the storm. Instantly I heard a soft lapping sound, no doubt caused by the fish. At the same moment, the halo of vaporous blue light that had confused me when

I woke in the middle of the previous night, because it had seemed so unreal, rose very slowly into the upper reaches of the hut. I was now able to make out the shape of Maram, since her white gown reflected the blue luminescence.

Suddenly I understood. How had I not thought of this earlier? Maram had given us sea light. The water in the tub emitted that same bluish light, verging on pale green, that I had seen three years before, in the middle of the night, during my first boat trip between the island of Saint-Louis and the island of Gorée. I had gone up on deck to escape the stifling heat of the hold, where Estoupan de la Brüe had put me, in contravention of all the laws of hospitality and humanity, despite knowing that I suffered from seasickness. When our ship stopped halfway between the continent and the island of Gorée, I was able to observe that natural phenomenon so often described by sailors accustomed to crossing the line of the tropics. Sometimes, in those sweltering climes, the sea glows from within, seeming to grant observers the strange ability to see all the hidden treasures of the abyss. So it was that my seasickness faded when I saw, gliding under the motionless ship, thousands of shapes sparkling like precious stones sewn into the weft of a carpet of light, and set with filaments of seaweed glistening silver and gold.

The idea that Maram had collected this phosphorescent saltwater to illuminate her hut at night only increased the tenderness I felt for her. I might not share her representation of the world, or believe in the existence of her *rab*—the chimera of one of those archaic religions in which man and nature are one—but I was exalted by the idea that we felt the same attraction for beautiful things, even if they had no use.

Because while the luminescence from the tub of seawater was fainter than an oil lamp or even a candle, it had a beauty that touched my soul.

Maram and I were equally sensitive to the mysteries of nature. She, to conciliate them; I, to penetrate them. It was one more reason to love her . . . if reason has anything to do with love.

XXIII

As silent and light as a feather falling from the sky, Maram came back to the bed and sat facing me. I was deeply moved by the innocent gift she apparently wanted to offer me by bathing us in the halo of that poetic light, that sky-blue smoke enveloped in night. And I was about to tell her in my meager Wolof that I felt something more than tenderness for her when, interrupting me, she began narrating her story again.

So I had to content myself with being, for her, nothing more than an attentive listener. She gave herself to me in words and I tried to understand why. Telling me the story of her life was a choice, an election, the sign of a predilection. Was it because I was so foreign, so other? Not only a man, but a white man at that. Perhaps I was doomed never to be anything more than a passing stranger, a momentary confidant. I felt like a confessor, a recipient for all her misfortunes, enabling Maram to throw them overboard, out of sight, to free herself of them forever.

"As soon as our dugout was on dry land, the white man disappeared and left me in the hands of those two warriors, ordering them to take me to the fort only when no one could see us, in the middle of the night. My two guards tied me to the trunk of an ebony tree, not far from the riverbank, and sat a few steps away from me to smoke their pipes and drink a few mouthfuls of alcohol. This moment seemed perfect for my *faru rab* to come and rescue me, but he did not appear. I imagined that the place where we found ourselves was too far from Sor for him to have the power to save me. But I did not surrender to despair. I continued to seek a means of escape. I was sitting on the ground with my back against the tree and my arms, tied at the wrists, encircling its trunk. Seydou Gadio and Ngagne Bass were paying no attention to me, so I tried to loosen the rope. Despite my efforts, I got nowhere and I decided to conserve my energy so I would be ready to flee whenever an opportunity presented itself.

"No such opportunity arose on the way to the fort, where, after a long walk, my two guards flung me into a damp, white-painted room and slammed shut the thick wooden door. I had never seen a door like that before. I lay there, on the ground, in the half dark, and continued to hope.

"Not long afterward, the door opened and an old woman appeared. Holding a candle, she approached me shyly, telling me not to get angry or upset. She was not there to hurt me; she was simply bringing me something to eat and drink, to wash myself with and to wear. A little girl followed her inside, carrying a calabash of couscous and mutton and an earthenware jug of cool water. After I had eaten the couscous and drunk some water, this very young child, whose face I could hardly make out in the candlelight, stripped off my dirty pagne. I was so exhausted, I let her do it. And the old woman continued to speak to me while the little girl washed me and dried me, and tried to attire me in a kind of unfamiliar, uncomfortable clothing which she called a 'dress.' I felt very constricted, and since the fabric came all the way down to my feet, I realized it would hinder my movements. This clothing, which covered most of my body, was cut from a shiny cloth decorated with large flowers of a species unknown to me. It was a prison dress, which they had made me wear to prevent me from running away.

"As soon as I was clothed, the old woman and the little girl slipped away and the two warriors returned. They led me to a stone staircase where I almost fell several times, so unaccustomed was I to moving inside that dress. When we were outside the fort, they threw that fishing net over me again to hide me from prying eyes. Then, seeing that its weight, added to the constraint imposed by the dress I wore, was causing me to stumble when I walked, they decided it was preferable, for reasons of speed, to wrap me in the net and carry me like a sack. I was only sixteen years old and I was lighter than I am today, but that did not prevent the two men from cursing the king of Waalo, who had sent them to serve this diabolical white man by the name of Estoub. They weren't slaves; they were warriors. They couldn't wait to be returned to the service of their king so they could wage war again.

"After copiously insulting one another, accusing each other of not shouldering enough of the burden, they suddenly fell silent. I could not see anything in the black night, but I heard them announce to a guard, without stopping, that they were transporting a package to the room of the white man, Estoub. It seemed to me that we were going up, and their feet began to walk upon a ground that no longer crunched like sand on the riverbank but echoed slightly like the skin of a drum. To judge from their movements and their slowed pace, we had entered a place where they had to bend down to move forward. Finally, they tossed me into a dark, cramped room without freeing me from the net that held me prisoner.

"For what felt like a long time I lay on a wooden floor that smelled strange even through the fishy stink of the net, whose layers of rope mesh close to my mouth made it hard for me to breathe.

"All of a sudden, I was startled by a commotion, raised voices. I must have fallen asleep, despite the discomfort of my position, because my vision was now flooded with light. The floor swaying under me and the sound of water brought me to the realization that I was in one of those enormous boats built by you white men, the masters of the sea. Perhaps I was being taken beyond the horizon to that place from which no Africans ever returned. I was on the verge of tears: it seemed to me that my home, the village of Sor, was lost to me forever."

Maram fell silent again, as if contemplating her own words. Sometimes, when we think back to our past and our old beliefs, we find ourselves in the presence of a stranger. That stranger is our former self. Even if he is always there, in our mind, he often escapes us. And when we find him again, in a half-forgotten memory, we see that other self in a different light; sometimes we feel indulgent toward him, sometimes angry, sometimes tender, and sometimes frightened, just before he vanishes again.

I projected these thoughts, which were mine, onto Maram. I imagined it was possible that she was thinking them at the same time I was, as if, in sad and serious moments, certain words have the power to induce the same state of mind in two attentive listeners. Or at least I hoped this with all my heart, because I loved Maram. But her story made me fear that she did not share my love. After all, I belonged to the race of her oppressors.

XXIV

In the dimness of the hut, I could not see Maram's eyes. Only the outlines of her face and her torso were visible to me, faintly luminescent. I loved her gentle, firm voice that filled my soul with its calmness. All languages, even the harshest, sound smoother and sweeter when spoken by women. And Wolof, which already struck me as a wonderfully tender language, sounded especially sublime to me coming from Maram's mouth.

I had reached the point where I was starting to forget my French. I was immersed in another world and the translation of Maram's words in my notebooks, my dear Aglaé, cannot convey the flashes of complicity that accompanied them. Perhaps I dreamed that she was speaking to me in a unique language, addressed solely to me, different from whatever words she might have used to communicate her story to anyone else. I sensed some undefinable spark of affection or friendship in the way she spoke to me which led me to hope that, despite all her misfortunes, she set me apart from other men, white or Black.

These subtleties do not appear in the account of Maram that I am giving you, Aglaé, and I can assure you that, if my translation of her words is not exact, it is because I am imbuing them with all the contradictory emotions that they provoke in me even now. I should add that Wolof has a concision that French lacks, and that sometimes what Maram expressed to me in a single striking phrase, the precise memory of which I have been able to retrieve, I have been obligated to transcribe in three or four sentences in French.

It is also true that Maram did not recount her story to me exactly in the way I am writing it down for you. But the more I write, the more I become a writer. Though sometimes, forgetting exactly what she told me, I have imagined what must have happened to her, that does not mean that I am lying. It seems to me fair to think now that only fiction, the novel of a life, can give a genuine glimpse of its profound reality, its complexity; only fiction can illuminate its darkest corners, which are often indiscernible even to the person whose life it was.

So Maram continued to tell me her sad tale and I am narrating it to you in the language that is common to both of us, my dear Aglaé, but which separates me from my youthful love. Here, then, is the rest of what she told me happened to her on Estoupan de la Brüe's ship, which I report to you in my own words.

"The door to the room in which I lay was opened and I heard footsteps coming toward me. A man's boot pushed me. It was the white man, Estoub. I couldn't see him but he was shouting between his teeth in that birdlike language of yours. He seemed furious and he left immediately, slamming the door behind him. Soon afterward, someone else entered and began freeing me from the fishermen's net that had been wound around me.

"This was no easy task. My rescuer was the same old woman who had looked after me inside the fort of Saint-Louis. When she had partly uncovered me, she let out a cry of terror. The mesh of the net had become so deeply embedded in the flesh of my cheeks and forehead that it looked as though half of my face was covered with fish scales, like ritual scarifications. I couldn't see myself, but I gathered, from what the old woman said, that my beauty had been destroyed and I had become repulsive. My eyes were puffy, swollen from the tears that I had been holding back ever since I had been dragged from the dugout by my abductors, and my tangled hair must have smelled of fish. The fabric of the dress they had put on me the previous day was covered with stains that obscured the printed flowers that decorated it.

"The old woman, who introduced herself to me as Soukeyna, began to weep as she undressed me. She kept repeating: 'My poor little girl, what have they done to you?' in such a plaintive tone that I almost wept myself. But I held back my tears because I did not want to show any sign of weakness. This woman, whose skin was as wrinkled as an old elephant's hide, was the servant of the white man, Estoub. She had fed, washed, and dressed me the night before so as to offer me to him in good condition. I was still very young, but I had already realized that in the new world I had been forced to enter, my purpose would be to give pleasure to the white master who had bought me for the price of a musket. And my uncle had showed him the use to which he could put me.

Perhaps the old woman, Soukeyna, was also weeping for her own fate, sensing that Estoub would be greatly displeased not to be able to possess me as soon as he wished.

"I do not know how Soukeyna described my state to Estoub, but he left me in peace for six days, during which time I was able to gather my strength through sleep, her care for me, and the abundant and varied food that she brought me every morning and evening. On the first day she washed my whole body and showed me the part of the room hidden by a small wooden screen where I could relieve myself: a sort of chair with a hole in it, from which she withdrew a little tub twice a day, pouring its foul contents into the sea.

"For the first three days, I slept like a log and I did not wake up until Soukeyna came in to look after me. She took particular care with my face and I guessed that as soon as she told Estoub it had been restored to its former state, he would come and visit me. I had made the decision not to speak to this woman and she did not seem put out by my silence, as if she feared adding another heavy load of remorse to her old memory, as if she feared the next load might be the one that finally broke her.

"I was starting to feel more like myself again by the fourth day, and I slept very little. I noticed that a little bit of light moved across a thick cloth hung high on the wall above my bed. I had heard waves behind that wall and had guessed, from the swaying of the 'ship,' as Soukeyna called it in French, that we were at sea. The truth of this intuition was confirmed when, kneeling on my bed, lifting up the cloth to reveal a piece of wood that I was able to slide sideways, I received a shower of saltwater directly in my face. My skin stung, because my wounds were still not healed, but that rush of sea air into the room where I had been confined for several days did me good. I took deep breaths, and this exercise—which I began performing from then on at any moment of the day or night—gave me back my courage.

"With a little more light, I could explore that room, which was far smaller than the hut in which we sit now, Adanson. It was there, no doubt, that the white man, Estoub, slept when he took the ship from the island of Saint-Louis to visit his brother in Gorée, as old Soukeyna had told me. Other than my bed, a small table, and a large trunk, I saw no other objects in that room, which must have been emptied of his belongings before I was locked inside.

"I had noticed that old Soukeyna opened the trunk every morning to take out the linen, which she must then have delivered to Estoub. But she locked it afterward, just as she did with the door that kept me prisoner. That wooden trunk was very big, covered in dark leather, its uprights strengthened by shiny nails with bulbous heads, hammered closely together in a row.

"On the sixth day, however, Soukeyna forgot to lock it. As soon as she had left the room, I slid back the wooden plank that opened my prison to the sea to give myself more light. In the daylight, the trunk's leather did not appear quite so dark. It had a sweet odor, like that of a flower. I knelt in front of it and raised its heavy lid.

"At first all I saw was a heap of white linen: stockings, shirts, breeches like yours, Adanson. Finding nothing interesting within, I was about to close the trunk out of fear that Soukeyna would come back and catch me looking through it, when I suddenly decided to empty it completely, just to make sure there was nothing useful in there. Beneath Estoub's white linen, I first discovered a small gold-colored iron stick with a round glass knob at one end, which I thought I would be able to steal without it being noticed. Next, I found a fairly long rope which, along with the previous object, would perhaps aid me in the escape I was starting to formulate in my mind.

"I had almost finished my search when I felt a strange texture under my fingertips. It was not cloth. Blindly I groped the surface of something soft, slightly oily, and vaguely uneven, concealed beneath one of Estoub's long tunics. I pushed aside Estoub's last remaining clothes and was stunned by what I saw.

"Lining the bottom of the trunk, folded neatly into seven layers, was the skin of my *rab*, my guardian demon. It was a deep black with pale yellow stripes in the same patterns as the pagne in which he had been clothed when he appeared to me in my dream, just before metamorphosing into a giant boa. I thought I would die of happiness and gratitude. So my *rab* had not abandoned me! He was still protecting me, even as I was taken farther and farther away from Sor! I felt certain that this discovery was no coincidence. My *rab* wasn't dead; he lived inside me, and with his aid I would survive.

"It hardly mattered how Estoub had come into possession of this enormous boa skin. Perhaps one of our kings had given it to him, as proof of the monstrousness of the local animals. Perhaps he had hunted it himself, or bought it from another hunter. The fact that Estoub kept it at the bottom of the trunk containing his own clothes demonstrated how highly he prized it, the care he took to prevent it from drying out or fading. But I had more of a right to that boa skin than he did. To him it was merely a ceremonial object, probably intended to make people believe he had hunted and killed a monster, whereas for me this skin was host to a soul that was twinned with mine. So I took it out of the trunk and wrapped myself in it, tying it to my body with the rope I had found in the same place. There was enough space underneath my bed to conceal the snakeskin, and I took care to let a pagne hang down to the floor to hide it from Soukeyna's sight.

"I had time after that to neatly rearrange the linen inside the trunk, hoping that the old woman would not notice anything was missing. She returned to lock it later that day, while I pretended to sleep, and I saw that she didn't bother opening the lid to check its contents.

"Late in the afternoon of the seventh day at sea, Soukeyna told me that we were close to the island of Gorée and that Estoub would come to my room that night. She had brought me a pretty dress, the same pearly, iridescent color as the inside of a large seashell in sunlight. I feigned pleasure at the sight of that dress, and Soukeyna, encouraged by my attitude, whispered that I should be kind to Estoub. The old woman added that giving him pleasure would be of great benefit to me. If I was to his taste, he would make me his principal concubine in Saint-Louis and, if I played my cards right, I could become rich enough to free myself from the need for any protector once he had returned to France or died. With all the wealth that I would have extorted from him, I would be able to buy myself a husband more to my liking and—why not?—avenge myself cruelly on the person who had sold me to Estoub.

"I let her talk because, having discovered that my *rab* was still looking after me, since I was in possession of his skin, I felt certain that the life of a concubine that Soukeyna was describing to me would not be mine. I was not born to be a slave, for Estoub or anyone else, and if one day I did take revenge on my uncle, it would not be thanks to the wealth that my beauty had allowed me to extract from a white man.

"Nodding my head almost imperceptibly, as if to suggest to Soukeyna that I was starting to accept this new fate, I put on a pair of what looked like white cloth breeches that came down to my knees, with a hole in their crotch. Then she helped me put on the shell-colored dress in such a way that I guessed her aim was to make it easy for Estoub to take it off. She did not tie the laces at my back, which was a big help to me later.

"Not long after sunset, the old woman returned with seven 'candles,' which she lit and placed in a large dish on the small table near the bed, whose 'sheets' she had changed. She gave me her advice, as—in her own words—a 'woman of the world.' No doubt she herself had been a white man's concubine in her youth.

"Soukeyna must have made extravagant promises to Estoub, because he was smiling broadly, revealing all his horrible teeth, that night when he entered the room where I had been kept prisoner for the previous seven days. But his smile did nothing to lessen the cruelty in his eyes and—as I lay waiting for him on the bed, the way Soukeyna had told me to—I had the same impression as I'd had the first time I saw him. He looked like he was about to devour me.

"Estoub was wearing a sort of white cotton hat tied under

his chin and a long shirt of the same color. In the candlelight his face glowed red, gradually becoming covered by little spots of blood under his skin. He started to stammer a few incomprehensible words while his hands moved toward my chest. But when he leaned down to grab my breasts, I smashed him in the left temple with the gold-colored iron stick I had found in his trunk, which I had kept hidden in my right hand, beneath a fold of my dress. The blow stunned him momentarily, giving me time to draw my legs to my chest while he leaned over me. I struck him very hard with the soles of my feet. My *rab* must have shared his strength with me at that moment, because Estoub's head banged violently against the low ceiling and he collapsed unconscious beside the bed.

"The first thing I did, even before getting rid of that dress, was to move Estoub's inert body out of the way so I could pull the snakeskin out from under the bed. Once I was naked, I took the rope that was wrapped around my *rab*'s rolled-up skin and tied it to my waist. Holding the skin in my arms, I blew out the seven candles and opened the door of my prison, which Estoub had not locked. It led to a corridor that ended with three steps. Fearing that Estoub's heavy fall might have aroused attention, I waited for a moment before running as quietly as possible to the stairs, which I quickly climbed. The rolled-up snakeskin did not hinder my progress. It was light and I felt as if I were flying.

"I found myself almost immediately in the open air, and, while I was ready to confront anyone who stood in my way—Soukeyna, a sailor, or one of Estoub's guards—I encountered nobody. It was as if the ship were deserted, or as if I had miraculously become invisible and inaudible.

"I hid behind a sort of large bundle near the edge of the ship. I looked up at the sky: from the position of the stars, I estimated that dawn was still a long way off. The moon was black, but to my right I could make out the shadow of an island that must have been Gorée. To my left, a great mass of dark earth blocked the horizon. But what struck me was the strange state of the sea. It glistened from within, radiating an opalescent light that gave me the impression, when I climbed down the ladder attached to the left side of the ship, that the world had been turned upside down. I was about to dive into a liquid sky, luminous and open, while leaving behind a place imprisoned in oppressive darkness.

"I had no fear of entering that sea like an inverted sky— like all the children of Sor, I had learned to swim in a *marigot* close to our village. Holding the rolled-up skin of my *rab* in one hand, and hoping that it would float for quite a long time before it became waterlogged, I began swimming toward Cap Vert. The land seemed all the darker to me since the sea was both translucent and phosphorescent. But, very luckily, nobody on the ship saw me in the water, because it was the last place they would have expected me to hide.

"Protected by my *rab*, I was not attacked by the sharks that infest the water on that coastline, feeding on the bodies of slaves who are thrown into the sea when they fall ill or who try to escape Gorée by swimming. I do not know what tribute my *rab* offered the genie of the ocean to save me from them, but a strong current quickly carried me in the direction of land.

"Suddenly the light in the sea was extinguished and it blended with the night. I could hear the sound of waves crashing softly on the shore. The high, dark wall of a forest slowly came closer while the skin of my totem was starting to sink into the water, dragging me down with it. After briefly being trapped in a mass of sea foam, I felt sand under my feet. And, despite the sharp-edged rocks that protected the beach and that might have torn me to pieces, I had enough strength, pulling on the rope that connected us, to save my *rab* from the sea's mouth.

"I collapsed onto the sand of a small beach very close to the great forest that I had discerned from the sea. After catching my breath, I hurried toward the line of trees to find shelter for my *rab* and myself. Before penetrating the forest, I had the feeling that I was about to enter a world of vegetation as dangerous as the sea's world of water. As I turned back to look at the shoreline of pale sand behind me, it appeared as a slender border between two different oceans, now equally dark.

"Before going farther in, I scanned the horizon and saw neither Estoub's ship nor the island of Gorée. Presumably the current had taken me even farther along the coastline than I had hoped. But I was afraid that Estoub, if he hadn't died from the blow to his head, would find a way to come after me. So I hid behind a tree, at the edge of the forest, and waited for day to break over the ocean.

"The sea was as naked as I was: its strangely smooth gray skin shivered, grazed at times by the wings of the great white birds that glided above it, watching for shoals of invisible fish. Their feathers caught and reflected the pink and gold hues of dawn. Their loud cries almost drowned out the immense, steady chant of the sea.

"Finally I balanced the rolled-up skin of my totem on top

of my head to free my hands and advanced into the forest. I was hungry and thirsty but I didn't stop walking. At first I moved as quickly as possible, but soon my stride grew weary, and I was on the edge of exhaustion. Had I still been near the village of Sor, I would have known where to find fruit to eat, and where to find the river or a *marigot* where I could quench my thirst. But there, in that forest of ebony trees that grew denser with every step I took, I lost my bearings. My head was spinning, my legs trembling; I felt close to fainting, but I couldn't stop. I had to put as much distance as possible between myself and Estoub's ship. But as the sun rose in the sky, the heat of that humid forest overpowered me and I had barely enough strength to hold the skin of my *rab* to my chest before curling up at the foot of a tree."

XXV

Maram fell silent once again, as if giving me time to steep in her words and absorb the meaning of her story. She seemed tranquil as I meditated on the possibility that I had perhaps been on Estoupan de la Brüe's ship while she was there too, three years earlier. Was it possible I hadn't seen her while I was taking the air on deck the night she dived into a luminous sea and swam to Cap Vert?

Our faces were still dimly lit by the luminescent seawater in the tub where the fish swam. I could hear them moving about softly. Why did Maram use that particular method to light her hut? Was it in memory of her escape from the ship belonging to Estoub, as she called the director of the Senegal Concession? I didn't dare ask any questions. I imagined that the answers would emerge from the rest of her story anyway, and I was right: I would soon learn the unbelievable, unexpected, violent truth.

"I was woken from the shallow sleep in which I floated," Maram went on, "by a calloused hand placed gently on my forehead. I half opened my eyes and saw, leaning over me, the very wrinkled face of an old woman who at first I thought must be Soukeyna. I cried out, but she reassured me in a quavering voice. With a big smile that revealed the single remaining tooth in her mouth, the old woman told me that her name was Ma-Anta. She had seen me in her dreams on each of the past seven nights and I was to become her secret daughter. I would look after her until the day she left, when I would replace her.

"I did not grasp the full meaning of her words. I thought it odd that she was talking about me looking after her when I was the one about to die of exhaustion. But Ma-Anta kept repeating that she had glimpsed me in her dreams, that I was her secret daughter.

"I had closed my eyes again when she slipped her hand under the back of my neck to raise my head and moisten my dried lips with a few drops of water. After that, still smiling but now silent, she handed me a piece of sugarcane and signaled that I should suck it. I sucked out the sap for a long time, until I had enough strength to stand up. Ma-Anta remained crouching on the ground beside me, and I realized that she was so old she could not get to her feet without aid. She did not look worried, however. She just crouched there, smiling, waiting for me to help her up. I did so, and was surprised by her lightness. She was no heavier than a child.

"And indeed there was something very childlike about Ma-Anta, who kept laughing joyously at everything. She told me to pick up from the ground a long staff enveloped in red leather and embedded with cowries, which, laughing, she called 'little brother.' She was still chuckling when she turned her back on me and began to limp away, her spine hunched, as slowly as a beetle climbing a sand dune in the Lompoul Desert.

"I put the rolled-up skin of my snake-totem on my head

again and followed her, attempting to copy the rhythm of her gait, so lacking in speed that I felt as if I were walking on the spot. A multitude of questions filled my mind. How could such a frail old woman have found me in the middle of nowhere in that forest of ebony trees where I had been wandering for hours? Where had she come from and where was she leading me? Was this Ma-Anta a real person or a figment of my imagination, one of those figures from tales who appear out of nowhere when all seems lost? Perhaps I was still lying, close to death, at the foot of the tree where I had collapsed. Perhaps Ma-Anta was merely the shadow of a final comfort offered to me by my *rab* in that forest so distant from our village of Sor and our native bushland.

"If my mind was questioning the reality of that improbable situation, following in the footsteps of a frail old woman in ocher-colored clothes, my aching body soon silenced it. No, I wasn't dying anymore. I was no longer lying with my neck resting on the root of an ebony tree. I was on my feet now, and I was desperately hungry and, above all, thirsty. But I had no right to complain or even sigh, because Ma-Anta, walking ahead of me, must have been suffering far more than I was. Every step she took appeared to demand an immense effort.

"She wore a pointed hat cut from the same ocher cloth as her tunic, and her neck arched down toward the ground. Behind her in the dust, Ma-Anta left an uninterrupted furrow— the evidence that her left foot never left the ground. Without my noticing, we had passed from the ebony forest to a forest of palm trees and date palms, which offered us less shelter from the sun. Ma-Anta's pace did not change, however: she was as relentlessly slow as always. I gritted my teeth as I followed her, relieved now that she was not going any faster, because I was running out of strength. I thought that she had foreseen, perhaps from the very beginning of our journey, that I would end up not being able to go any faster than this.

"Before I even got to know her, I was struck by the impression that there was a sort of lesson, something to be meditated upon, in all of her actions and her kindness toward me. She had fallen silent—she who had been so talkative when she first found me—and walked without lifting her eyes from the ground. I felt as though I should imitate her, even trailing my left leg in the dirt, following in her footsteps so exactly that had I had the strength to turn around, I wouldn't have been able to distinguish my footsteps from hers.

"Just as the endless beating of a tambour puts you into a trance, Ma-Anta taught me—this was her first lesson—that marching with the same steady rhythm numbs the pain of the body. And when I abruptly emerged from this strange sort of trancelike lethargy, perhaps upon a sign sent to me by my *rab*, who was anxious about me, night had fallen and I was still walking slowly behind Ma-Anta in the forest of palm trees and date palms which we had entered in daylight.

"Returning to consciousness in that way, I was once again aware of all the pains in my body, and I was close to weeping when Ma-Anta suddenly came to a halt. A lion and a hyena were lying in our path, and were it not for their foul stench—a sickening mix of blood and viscera from all their prey—hitting the back of my throat, I would have thought I was once again the prisoner of a dream within a dream.

"The lion and the hyena, that strange pair of enemy beasts, remained motionless, not even deigning to look at us. When

Ma-Anta started walking again, the two animals, instead of leaping upon us and devouring our flesh, calmly moved aside before escorting us to the old woman's hut in the village of Ben.

"Ma-Anta was a healer, and she was the one who completed my initiation. She forged the woman I have become. She explained who my *faru rab* was and how I should coexist with him, avoid offending him or making him jealous of me. Ma-Anta taught me a few offerings I could make to him to keep him on my side. She taught me how to look after his skin so that it did not lose its beautiful colors of deep black and pale yellow.

"I arrived in this village three rainy seasons ago, and Ma-Anta's influence over the villagers was so strong that they believed her when she told them that she was taking over my body and abandoning hers because it was too old. Since she never left her hut anymore, I would treat the villagers who came to seek care in the courtyard of her enclosure, hidden beneath the skin of my totem, limping and made up to look like her.

"At first I would return to the hut where Ma-Anta lay in bed and report to her exactly what the villagers were asking for. She taught me to listen. She often repeated that the first remedies are to be found in the words of the patients describing the symptoms of their illness. The plant extracts that she pointed out to me would have had no power to heal had they not been accompanied by healing words, because man is man's first remedy.

"It was with her tender words that Ma-Anta healed my invisible wounds. As she also told me repeatedly, one must be healed oneself before one can heal others. But Ma-Anta must have healed me imperfectly, because, not long after her departure, I remembered all the pain that my uncle had caused me. And while, day after day and night after night, I fought to free myself from the idea, and in defiance of the advice of my *rab*, who opposed it in my dreams, I decided to take my revenge upon him."

Maram had expressed her desire for vengeance in a voice so soft and calm that I thought I must have misunderstood. She appeared discordant to me, a whispering woman with a firmness of soul revealed by the terrible story of her life.

I was twenty-six and I had faith in the philosophy and science of my century. For me, what Maram called, in Wolof, *faru rab* was nothing more than a chimera. I did not question the existence of the boa, whose skin, which she wore, must have been close to twenty feet long—or just over six meters, in the new imperial metric. I had even heard it said by some Africans that there were snakes near Podor, a village on the Senegal River, that measured about forty feet and were capable of swallowing a cow. But what I could not accept—because of my understanding of the world, which I considered superior to hers—was that Maram should lend this animal mystical powers and believe that it was protecting her. Now, however, as I write her story, trying desperately to remember what she said to me in Wolof, I am no longer so certain that reason remains triumphant. And I say that because of something, my dear Aglaé, that you will soon discover in the account that follows.

XXVI

I did not share Maram's beliefs, which I thought superstitious, but I would eagerly have shared my life with her. Could we have lived happily together? Wouldn't I have been tempted, after marrying her, to make her more acceptable to other Europeans by replacing her beliefs with my own? To persuade the world I came from to forgive me for marrying a Black woman, wouldn't I have tried to take away her snakeskin, to teach her to speak French, to carefully instruct her in the precepts of my religion?

Even though her beauty and her ideas of the world, inseparable from her as an individual, had been the first sources of my love for her, my prejudices would have perhaps led me to try to "whiten" her. And if Maram, out of love for me, had agreed to become a white Black woman, so to speak, I am not certain that I would have continued to love her. She would have become a shadow of herself, a simulacrum. Wouldn't I ultimately have missed the real Maram, just as I miss her today, fifty years after losing her?

I did not formulate these questions about a potential marriage with Maram as precisely then as I do now in my written account for you, Aglaé. Perhaps they would have become clearer if my existence had taken the path that my deep love for her urged it to take. Maram had a greater influence over me than I would have ever imagined. And if I chose you, Aglaé, to be my silent confidante in the face of my coming death, it is because I sought to ease the pain in my soul with healing words, just as Maram's words did for so many others.

After telling me in her soft voice about her decision to take revenge on her uncle, Maram went back to her story. She sat perfectly still in the faint, wavering light and I had to lean forward slightly to hear her. It was almost as if she was ashamed to speak loudly.

"I started to think about my vengeance after Ma-Anta's departure.

"One morning, Ma-Anta announced that the time had come for her to leave for the forest where she had found me. She was going to disappear into the woods, and I was not to go looking for her body. Her final wish was that I should pick up her staff, which was imbued with mystical powers, seven days after her departure, in a location that she would not reveal to me. It was up to me to find it on my own. But I wasn't to worry, because it would be a simple task: all I had to do was follow her tracks.

"I begged her not to abandon me, kept telling her she had not finished teaching me all her secrets, but she refused to listen. She just shook her head, smiling, exposing without shame her sole tooth, the last vestige of a long and mysterious life of which she had never revealed a single episode. 'You know more than I do now,' she said each time I tried to delay her departure.

"And at dawn on one empty day, after telling me when I should leave fish on the roof of the hut for the lion and the hyena, her two *rabs*, she left. I watched her through my tears until she vanished behind the first row of date palms in the Krampsanè Forest. Without her, my breath of life shrank to almost nothing, until I was merely a body without a soul. I missed the light touch of her hand on my head in blessing, which I had felt every morning when I knelt in front of her.

"Seven days later, I obeyed her instructions and went off in search of the staff she called her 'little brother.' I found it under an ebony tree. It wasn't difficult: I simply had to follow the furrow that the staff had left behind on the ground. Despite the week that had passed since her departure, the furrow had not been erased. I placed my feet in her footprints, sensing the effort she had expended to advance under sun and moon, imagining her using up the last of her strength in that voyage of no return.

"Back in Ben with Ma-Anta's mystical staff, I thought again about Baba Seck. He was my past, as painful as a suppurating wound. The old healer was no longer there to help me erase from my memory that fatal instant when my uncle had tried to penetrate my young girl's body as if I had been a consenting, fully grown woman. My rage surged back like those waves, always bigger and angrier on stormy days, that pulverize the heaviest dugouts, sending fragments of wood flying in all directions.

"I was haunted by one particular image of him. I saw him running away, carrying the musket that Estoub had given him in exchange for me, and not even glancing at me, as if I disgusted him. I was constantly assailed by that memory, which was destroying my spirit. Perhaps I would regret not listening to the voice of my *rab* when he advised me to forgive my uncle all the evil he had done to me, but I had already made up my mind: I was going to punish him.

"There was a man here who I knew would not refuse to serve me, because I had saved his daughter's life. Senghane Faye was young and intrepid. I believed I could trust him to go to the village of Sor and deliver my message word for word. I wanted my words to haunt and hurt my uncle as much as his actions haunted and hurt me. There are words that heal and others that can kill slowly. My uncle would be the only person there who would understand the meaning of the message that Senghane delivered. Out of fear that the truth would be revealed, that his shame would become visible to all, I knew he would attempt to erase me from the world so that the story of my disappearance that he had no doubt invented would continue to appear true. I knew too that my threat of misfortune being brought down upon the village if anyone tried to find me would attract him here to Ben like a moth to a flame. I did not imagine that other butterflies—like you, Michel Adanson—would come here too and burn their wings.

Hearing my name in Maram's mouth, I felt myself blush. My role in her story was hardly a heroic one. I had walked onstage uninvited to play a part that was not mine to play. My curiosity had perhaps thwarted her plan to avenge herself on her uncle. But at the same time, I liked the way Maram pronounced my name. It sounded a little like "Misséla Danson," as if the peculiarly sweet and gentle accents of Wolof had—perhaps involuntarily on her part—hinted at her first stirrings of affection for me.

"To start with," she went on, "I thought you had been sent here either by my uncle or by Estoub, but that seemed impossible because, unless you were a man of no consequence in their eyes, neither of them would have told you about their attempt to rape me. I was seized with doubt when I saw in your escort Seydou Gadio, the warrior from Waalo who accompanied Estoub the day my uncle sold me for his musket. But this Seydou Gadio cannot have recognized me disguised as I—"

Maram did not finish her sentence. I caught a glimpse of her abruptly standing up in the bluish darkness, then moving over to a dark corner of the hut where I could no longer see her. I listened and was about to get up in turn when she whispered to me not to move under any circumstance, no matter what I might see. Her order, though delivered in a murmur, was so forceful that I obeyed it unthinkingly. And I am very glad I did, because if I hadn't I would have lost my life that night in Maram's hut.

As commanded, I stayed perfectly still. Outside the hut, everything seemed normal. Nighttime in Senegal is a discordant concert of cries, moans, and hoots from animals great and small, hunting or hunted, which—through force of habit—one ends up no longer hearing. Behind this formidable background noise, I could perceive nothing strange until I thought I heard someone running fast, getting closer.

Seconds later, the woven rush mat that covered the entrance to Maram's hut was knocked down by two or three blows of such violence that the entire edifice seemed to totter. Dazzled by the light from a lamp which struck me at first as very bright, because my eyes were used to the darkness, I gradually made out the shadow of a tall man standing in front of me. He took a step forward, then stopped. And I thought I recognized Baba Seck.

In his left hand, Maram's uncle was holding up an oil lamp, moving it in various directions so that its flickering flame would illuminate the inside of the hut. In his right hand he held a musket, its silver decorations gleaming softly. He stared at me with dead eyes. He looked exhausted. This man who had always welcomed me to his village dressed in the finest robes, his small white beard neatly trimmed, was now in rags, his hair and beard overgrown, with no shoes on his feet, the lower part of his legs covered in red dust.

After poisoning us with curiosity by telling us the story of the revenant, Baba Seck must have followed Ndiak and myself all the way from Saint-Louis to Cap Vert. Braving a thousand dangers so as not to lose us from sight, he must have walked alongside the Lompoul Desert and stopped in Meckhé, Sassing, and Keur Damel. He must, like us, have crossed through the Krampsanè Forest and hidden at the edge of it while Maram tended to me. He looked as though he had not eaten anything for several days.

"Where is she?" he asked me in a strangled voice.

I thought about asking him who he was talking about, but decided that such a response would have been inappropriate. We both knew he was asking about Maram. She was at the heart of his life and of mine. Since I said nothing, he was distracted by the lapping sound emanating from the tub of water at the hut's entrance. Forgetting me, he put his lamp on the ground and took a step to the side so he could lean over the tub. And while he examined the surface of the water, trying to understand what was moving under it, I saw a huge shadow peel itself slowly from the upper reaches of the hut, just above his head.

I was petrified. I tried to cry out, to warn Baba Seck of the danger that was closing in on him, but no sound emerged from my throat. Death was approaching and he did not sense it coming. It was an enormous animal that seemed to float through the air of the hut. I glimpsed its triangular head, almost as big as Baba Seck's own skull, and a thin, black, forked tongue darting in and out, as if from its wide closed mouth a small, two-headed snake was trying to escape, being sucked back in each time. Jet black with pale yellow stripes, the skin of the boa gleamed in the orange light of the oil lamp on the ground.

Maram's uncle, unaware of the danger above him, was still leaning over the tub of seawater whose function, in a flash of intelligence, I suddenly grasped: it was there not only to illuminate the hut at night with its bluish light, but to serve as the boa's larder. Maram fed the beast on fish, offering it the pleasure of hunting them itself by plunging its head into the water, the rest of its giant body hanging from a few beams on the inside of the hut's roof. But this time, Maram was sacrificing not a fish to her boa, but a man. A man who, ignorant of the threat gliding closer and closer, was wondering what this tub was for, just as I had done several times that night.

The boa's head slowly inched toward the man's. And, with that instinct shared by all living beings when they are prey to mortal danger—which they can sense without yet seeing it—Baba Seck glanced at me. I do not know if the light from the lamp on the ground was bright enough for him to make out the terror that was deforming my features or if he was surprised by the direction of my gaze, but he finally looked up. And at the very moment when he stared at his death, it fell upon him and coiled itself around him.

Perhaps Baba Seck thought he had time to fire a musket shot at the boa. But the beast knocked him to the ground and fell on top of him with all its weight, and the bullet that sped from the musket did not hit its target. It grazed my head before bursting through the wall of the hut behind me.

In falling onto the man, the snake had overturned the lamp, which had gone out. And in the faint phosphorescent glow coming from the tub of seawater, I thought I could see a dark, twisting wave undulating at length across the floor. Before I fainted, I heard Baba Seck's bones snap one by one, like twigs crushed underfoot. Cries, moans, and then only gurgling.

XXVII

I had left my body during Baba Seck's death. And by fainting I had probably saved myself from a sudden stroke, something that often occurs to monkeys and men unlucky enough to encounter a boa.

Of course, Maram had set the giant snake not on me but on her uncle. Her order to remain motionless no matter what had saved me. Maram had had time to observe the monster's nature. A boa has very weak vision; its tongue acts as its nose and it is able to spot its prey only when the prey moves. Providence had decreed that my stillness would be prolonged by the fear that paralyzed me when I caught sight of the boa. And it was also that same stillness which had saved me from Baba Seck's bullet.

When I woke, I was no longer in Maram's hut but in the open air. I was lying under an ebony tree. Despite the heat, I felt cold. My neck was stiff and painful, as was the rest of my body. Fleeting images of Baba Seck's horrific death kept flashing through my mind. I was still afflicted with that animal fear which, since the beginning of time, has appeared unique to each of its victims but is actually the same for all of them.

When death catches an animal after a long chase, its

muscles stiffen like armor. The predator's first task, after killing its prey, is to release the tension in the dead animal's flesh with the ferocity of its teeth and claws or the massive pressure of its coiled body. I hoped that Baba Seck had been lucky enough to lose consciousness before feeling his muscles, the last remaining fortification of his body, crushed by the boa's torsions.

It was only when Ndiak, sitting close to me, gently put his hand on my shoulder that I was able to relax. By an irony of fate, the first words I spoke to him were the last words that had come from Baba Seck's mouth:

"Where is she?"

Since the Wolof language does not distinguish, in such an interrogative phrase, between masculine and feminine, Ndiak wasn't sure how to respond.

"The old healer? She's vanished. On the other hand, if you're talking about him, we found the twisted remains of a man inside the healer's hut. There's a foot stuck to what must have been his chest, a smashed eyeball in one hand, his tongue hanging out, his head turned to pulp, his guts spilled on the floor. It's not a pretty sight, believe me. And the stench! Do you know who it is?"

Without waiting for my answer, Ndiak told me how he, Seydou Gadio, and the others had come running from the other side of the village as soon as they'd heard the gunshot echo through the dawn. It had not taken them long to find me inside the healer's hut, white as a cotton flower, curled up on a bed, not far from the misshapen corpse that they had had to step over to carry me outside. Having made sure I was still alive, Seydou Gadio had gone back into the hut to inspect it.

He had come back holding a musket, no doubt the one that had fired the bullet that alerted them. Seydou had strode past the others, his face like an iron mask, heading quickly toward the Krampsanè Forest and ordering the others not to follow him or to enter the hut, where there might still be an enormous boa.

Surprised by the anxious look on my face, Ndiak tried to reassure me by explaining that I owed my life to Seydou Gadio. It was he who'd had the idea of placing a mirror in front of my mouth to find out if I was still alive, and he too who had designed a makeshift stretcher on which they had transported me from Keur Damel to the old healer's hut in Ben. He was my savior.

I let him speak. Ndiak could not have known that Seydou Gadio had recognized his old musket, the one that Estoupan de la Brüe had forced him to hand over in exchange for Maram.

"Is he going to kill her?" I said at last, interrupting his long encomium on Seydou Gadio.

"Kill the old healer?"

"No, the revenant. Maram Seck."

Incredulous, Ndiak made me repeat this.

"Yes, Maram Seck was the woman hiding inside that black and yellow snakeskin. Maram Seck, niece of Baba Seck, chief of the village of Sor!"

Ndiak was silent for a moment, as if seeking clues in his memory that might have enabled him to guess the old healer's true identity. But nothing came to him and he had to admit that, like me, he had been unable to identify Maram under her disguise. Since I kept asking about Maram with obvious anxiety, Ndiak assured me that Seydou was not going to kill her. He was a hunter who would not take any life without the necessary mystical protections. The very powerful spirit that had inhabited the hut was something to be feared and handled carefully.

Ndiak's words calmed me. Although such superstitions seemed irrational to me, they would at least prevent Seydou Gadio from killing Maram if he managed to find her in the Krampsanè Forest. The old warrior, just like Ndiak, had a conception of the world in which a man's life was inextricably linked to that of his protective *rab*. In their minds, Maram and the snake that had crushed Baba Seck to death were one and the same entity. Killing Maram would bring her *rab*'s wrath down on Seydou.

I asked Ndiak for something to drink and he told the others to bring me food too.

Before telling him Maram's story, in more or less the same words she had used when recounting it to me through a good part of the previous night, I noted that the desire and love she had inspired in me in such a brief time had not been extinguished.

Probably any other man would have been so horrified by Baba Seck's death that he would, in his terror, have confused Maram with the boa she had trained to kill her uncle. What a white man's reason might not have allowed him to think, his imagination would have forced him to feel: fear and disgust for the murderous snake-woman. For myself, however, I believed that Maram's vengeance was proportional to the crime her uncle had committed against her. Because while his rape of her had not been consummated, his attempt had destroyed the order of her world. Her uncle's act had crushed her life. That Maram should have crushed Baba Seck in the coils of her snake-totem seemed to me a form of poetic justice.

I was deep in these reflections when the villagers from Ben brought us a calabash of shark couscous, a dish I had not enjoyed when I first arrived in Senegal but which I had learned to love. I would never have believed it if someone had made such a prediction before my voyage, just as I would never have thought I might fall madly in love with a Senegalese woman. It seemed to me that, after three years in Senegal, I had become African in all my tastes. This was due not simply to force of habit, as might seem evident, but because, through speaking Wolof, I had come to forget that I was a European. I had not spoken French in several weeks, and the prolonged effort that had accustomed my tongue to pronouncing foreign words struck me as identical to that which had led me to enjoy the taste of foreign dishes and fruit.

Ndiak waited patiently for me to finish my meal. Following the custom of the country, I washed my right hand—the one I used exclusively to put food in my mouth—in a small calabash of pure water that they had brought me. Then I leaned back against the trunk of the ebony tree under which I had come to after fainting an hour earlier. And I began to tell Ndiak, in a low voice so as not to be overheard by our escort nor by the nearby villagers, the story told to me by Maram Seck.

It did not take much—a misplaced word, a hesitation between two phrases—for Ndiak to see Maram as a monster. On several occasions I thought I could read terror and incredulity in his eyes. In a gesture associated with a form of onomatopoeia that belongs, as far as I am aware, only to the Wolofs of Senegal, he kept tapping the fingertips of his right hand against his mouth and repeating something that sounded like: "*Shaaay Taytay, Shaaay Taytay.*" This mark of astonishment worried me because I wanted to win Ndiak over to Maram's side. He must see her not as a murderess but as the victim of the two men who had abused her: first her uncle, who had been perverse enough to try to possess her, and then Estoupan de la Brüe, who had bought her with Seydou Gadio's musket so he could try to succeed where Baba Seck had failed. In this attempt at narrative seduction, I chose not to hide from Ndiak the fact that I loved Maram. Because, if it was true that he was my friend, then—despite his fear of her—surely he would help me to save her from the punishment that Seydou Gadio would undoubtedly inflict on her if he found her in the forest.

So I set out to present Maram to Ndiak as a very beautiful young woman with whom I was madly in love, going so far as to admit that I had seen her naked, so that he would find it easier to understand the urge that drew me to her—like most young men of his age, Ndiak could hardly distinguish between lust and love. I also chose to lie about the way Baba Seck's death had occurred. I did not hide from Ndiak what struck me as plausible: that Maram had trained an enormous snake to kill her uncle. But I told him that, before fainting from fear at the hideous spectacle of Baba Seck's final moments, I had distinctly seen Maram run outside through the entrance of the hut. That was false, but it seemed important to me that Ndiak should not be in any doubt on this point.

"*Shaaay Taytay* . . . Are you sure, Adanson, that you saw Maram leave the hut while the boa was killing her uncle?"

I stated several times that I was absolutely certain. Moreover, this did not seem much of a lie to me, since, although I had not seen her leave the hut with my own eyes, I did not doubt that Maram had done so while I was unconscious.

But Ndiak, who had listened to all this very carefully, asked me to return to a moment in the story that struck him as implausible: Maram's escape from Estoupan de la Brüe's ship.

"But, Adanson, if what Maram told you is true, how did she manage to get away from the ship without being seen? I saw that ship in Saint-Louis and I know that there are always one or two sailors on duty whose job it is to patrol the deck, even in the middle of the night. Maram couldn't have dived off that ship without being . . . *Shaaay Taytay!*"

The image that flashed through Ndiak's mind was so monstrous to him that he couldn't finish his sentence. Yet again, I had to lie, altering the story that Maram had told me. So I said that she had stepped over a sleeping sailor, who was lying across the top of the small staircase that led to the ship's deck. And that the power of the current that had swept her away was such that, despite the other sailors being alerted by the sound of the splash when she dove into the sea, they had not dared lower a lifeboat into the water to follow her.

I was surprised by how easily I was able to embroider these imaginary adventures onto the tapestry of Maram's story. I understood Ndiak's questions. I would have asked them of Maram myself had I dared interrupt her. But the episodes of the story she had told me were so smoothly interlinked that I felt it would have been impossible to break that chain without running the risk of perturbing her. I recognized that I had been entranced by her account and that I had unthinkingly swallowed some of its inconsistencies. But I had to smooth them over now so that Ndiak would remain my ally in defense of Maram.

So I did not mention the way that, in Maram's version of her story, the old healer Ma-Anta, guided by a premonitory dream, had found her on the verge of death in the middle of a vast forest. Nor did it seem advisable to me to repeat Maram's claim that she and Ma-Anta had been escorted to the village of Ben by a lion and a hyena. That episode had made me think of those early paintings of the Garden of Eden in which the animals, even those most hostile to one another by nature, live in peace and harmony together. And I thought I had been right to stay silent about that episode when, soon after this, Ndiak told me that he had seen with his own eyes, at the edge of the Krampsanè Forest, while I was still lying unconscious on the makeshift stretcher, a lion and a hyena, side by side, delicately picking up between their jaws a fish that had been left to dry on the roof of a hut in the village of Ben. The hut belonging to Ma-Anta and Maram.

XXVIII

Musket slung over his shoulder, Seydou Gadio walked a few steps behind her, apparently unconcerned by the possibility that Maram would run away.

He had found her far to the north, near the borders of the Krampsanè Forest. It had been a simple task: her tracks had been particularly obvious. Beside her footprints, he had followed the continuous line left in the earth by the tip of a staff that she had dragged along the ground, as if she wanted to be followed. Sitting with her back against a tree—the only ebony tree among all the palm trees and date palms in that forest—she had told him she'd been waiting for him and that if he would allow her to bury the staff under the ebony tree, she would follow him afterward without offering any resistance. Seydou had agreed, and once the staff—which the warrior described as being covered with red leather and embedded with cowries—was underground, she had begun walking back to the village of Ben.

She was all I saw. Maram was dressed in an indigo and white tunic that came down to her ankles. Beneath this open-sided tunic was the same white one-piece she had been wearing the previous evening. Her hair was hidden under a scarf whose knot, covered in the folds of the pale yellow cloth, was invisible. Head held high, she passed in front of me without glancing in my direction. There was something ethereal about the way she walked; I had the impression that she was gliding above the earth.

My heart was pounding. I felt both disappointed and relieved that she had not looked at me. What could her eyes have told me? I was filled with the crazed hope that they would shine with the same love I felt for her. But why should she love me? I was no different from other men, except for the color of my skin, which she probably found as detestable as most Europeans find the skin of Africans. I was suffering. I was in the grip of a searing passion for Maram and it seemed impossible to me that she could feel the same way. It was absurd to imagine that, if she ever did love me, her love would be as spontaneous as mine, that it would enter her heart without warning, without concessions, without some kind of internal debate. Maram's life was hardly the ideal breeding ground for love at first sight. All her misfortunes had been brought about by men who had tried to make her the object of their pleasure. Wasn't it likely that she would consider my advances to be driven by nothing more than carnal desire, no sooner sated than forgotten? To prove to her—and perhaps to myself too—that the love I felt for her was not simply lust, I would need time. I wished I could court her with delicacy and patience, the kind of attentions inspired by the desire to be liked by one's beloved. But Providence decided otherwise, and its primary instrument was the intransigence of the chief of our escort.

Seydou Gadio, the man who had saved my life at Keur Damel, had immediately recognized his old musket lying next to the disfigured corpse in Maram's hut. It was the same weapon that had been swapped for a very young girl on the orders of Estoupan de la Brüe three years before. Although she had grown into a woman during that time, he had remembered her features and her gracefulness as soon as he saw her under the ebony tree. And if a man's dead body had been found in her hut, she had to be directly or indirectly responsible for his death. There was a strong chance that she had wished to avenge herself on the man who had tried to rape her, something that he, Seydou Gadio, had seen with his own eyes, as had his acolyte Ngagne Bass and Estoupan de la Brüe, while the three of them had been hunting in the bush near the village of Sor. Not to mention that the dead man had sold her into slavery for the price of a musket. Consequently, Seydou saw no reason not to return the young woman to her owner, M. de la Brüe. And to do this, he planned to take her to M. de Saint-Jean, the governor of Gorée, who would find a way to restore her to his brother's possession.

No matter how hard I tried to explain to Seydou—without revealing to him, as I had to Ndiak, that she was the dead man's niece—that a young woman of Maram's size could not possibly have enough strength to crush a man like that, and that the murderer was a boa, the old warrior showed no interest in my opinion.

Indeed, Seydou Gadio, who was not used to being contradicted, became angry when I told him we should leave Maram in peace in the village of Ben. His rage grew so great that he threatened me with his musket, yelling that he would shoot me if I tried to stop him doing his duty. Ndiak managed to calm him down a little. That did not prevent Seydou from warning the villagers who had gathered around us that if they attempted to keep Maram in Ben, there would be terrible reprisals. But the villagers, who had grown restless since the return of the woman whom they imagined to be an avatar of Ma-Anta, protested that Seydou did not have the authority to take her away. Ben was not part of the kingdom of Waalo, but of Kayor. The king of Kayor, the *damel*, was represented in Cap Vert by seven Lebu elders who met once a month in the village of Yoff to rule on the cases brought before them. The villagers promised to take their healer to Yoff the next day so that the seven wise men could decide what ought to be done.

The most outspoken of the villagers was Senghane Faye, whose daughter Maram had healed and whom she had sent to Sor as a messenger to lure her uncle to Ben. Senghane Faye was no professional warrior, but he held an assegai and menaced Seydou with it. For his part, the gray-haired warrior made clear that he would have no qualms about shooting Senghane in the head if he overstepped the mark.

Amid the uproar that followed this dispute, Maram—who until then had remained silent—suddenly raised her voice, catching me off guard, because I had been thinking that this moment was an opportunity to distinguish myself in her eyes.

"In the name of Ma-Anta, I ask you to listen to me," she shouted. "You are good people. Not one of you has ever asked me to perform an act of magic hostile to another during the two years that I assisted Ma-Anta here. Your true healer found me while I was wandering in the Krampsanè Forest three years ago. She chose me as her disciple. And since she left to seek repose in the forest one year ago, I, Maram Seck, have been your healer. A crime was committed in your village and I am responsible for it. If evil has entered the village of Ben, it is my fault. So I ask you to let this man, Seydou Gadio, take me wherever he deems fit and not to prevent him saving you from the person who has destroyed the harmony of your lives."

These words were enough to calm the villagers, who returned to their usual occupations. Only Senghane Faye seemed hesitant to obey the order she had given to let her leave. But she gave him a look, which I happened to see, that convinced him too to abandon her to her fate.

And so I was now the only one who wanted to prevent Seydou Gadio from taking Maram to the island of Gorée. It was the island of slaves, the most dangerous place in the world for her, the first step on the path toward a punishment whose violence I could all too easily foresee. If what she had told me about her encounter with Estoupan de la Brüe was true, I knew that the director of the Senegal Concession would avenge himself one hundredfold for such an offense, particularly since it had been inflicted upon him by a Black woman. My distress was intensified by Maram's refusal to look at me, as if she would not give me even the slightest encouragement to oppose the will of Seydou Gadio. How I wished she would give me a look as harsh as the one she had shot at Senghane Faye. At least I would have been worthy of her disapproval, which seemed to me a thousand times better than her indifference. I did not know enough about life at that point to realize that the discipline with which Maram displayed her indifference toward me might paradoxically have been a sign that she had feelings for me after all. When I did understand this, it was too late for her to confirm to me in words what her actions might have revealed to me if only I had been more perceptive.

I could not think of a way to help Maram without her

assent. Any hope I had of saving her from punishment for the murder of her uncle, to which she had tacitly confessed, was given to me by Ndiak. He signaled for me to join him away from the others.

"Listen, Adanson. Old Seydou Gadio isn't going to change his mind. So I've decided to go and ask my father to pardon Maram Seck. According to the slave code, she doesn't belong to Estoupan de la Brüe anymore, since she succeeded in escaping from him more than a year ago. My father has the right to pardon her because she is his subject, as was Baba Seck. The king of Kayor and the seven elders who represent him in Cap Vert have no jurisdiction here because Maram's uncle is from the village of Sor, which belongs to the kingdom of Waalo. So I'm going to ride hard to Nder, our capital, following the coast road from Keur Damel to Saint-Louis. I promise you that, with the speed of my horse, Mapenda Fall, I will bring you a response, good or bad, within seven days at the most. As for you, go with Seydou and Maram to Gorée. It is better for her if you don't leave her."

This plan struck me as madness, but it was the only hope of saving Maram to which I could cling. I was grateful to Ndiak for trying to persuade his father, whom he did not like, to show mercy in a way that no one could reasonably expect of him based on his comportment since the start of his reign. But I was also worried about my young friend. His journey would put him in danger because Ndiak intended to ride alone, and I felt sure that his horse would be coveted by every warrior he encountered on the way to Nder.

When I said this to him, he shrugged. He wasn't afraid. He would borrow my musket. No one would dare to attack him if he was armed.

"There is one thing I should mention, which you may not like," he added. "I will have to reveal Maram's true identity. I'll have to explain to my father that her own uncle, the chief of the village of Sor, tried to rape her. It is only at the price of that awful truth that she may be pardoned. We are exposing her family to a public shame that, from what you have told me, Maram wishes to avoid. If you save her, you will destroy her reputation and you will lose her love, because she will never be able to love the man who allowed the dishonor of the Secks in the village of Sor to become widely known."

I did not think long about this. I loved Maram too much to abandon her to a punishment that might end with her death, and I loved her enough to want her to live, even estranged from me, even if it meant she hated me for the way we had tried to save her. So I told Ndiak that Maram's life was more important to me than her family honor.

Ndiak went over to Seydou Gadio and told him his plan to ride to Nder to ask for a pardon for Maram, although he did not reveal her identity to the warrior. And, after gathering a few provisions and storing them in his horse's English saddle, that saddle which the king of Kayor had given to him in Meckhé, he rode away at a trot. My heart ached as I watched him disappear into the Krampsanè Forest.

I had known him as a child, and now he was a man. I knew perfectly well that nothing good could come of his decision. Out of friendship for me, he was risking his chances of one day becoming king. Even if that possibility was forbidden by the laws of succession in the kingdom of Waalo, Ndiak had made clear to me that he aspired to that title to bring honor to his mother, Mapenda Fall. But he would be mocked, and his sanity would be questioned, when the others learned that he had come all that way to ask the king, his father, to pardon a young woman who had murdered her own uncle. If he had done such a thing on his own account, it might have been put down to the folly of youth. The king would have pardoned Maram, on the assumption that his son would make her a concubine before soon growing weary of her. The request might have been dismissed as the passing whim of a young prince who had fallen in love for the first time. The griots would have sung of his perilous voyage to rescue a slave from her punishment as a somewhat ludicrous but still touching exploit. It would have become part of the legend of his rise to power, planting the seed in the minds of his rivals that he was intrepid—the most important quality of any young pretender to the throne.

But what would they think when they learned that he had exposed himself to so many dangers to ask his father to pardon a young woman for the benefit of another man, particularly when that other man was white? He risked becoming a laughingstock. Wouldn't those griots, who might have sung of his budding glory, instead present him, privately or publicly, as a son unworthy of his father, a servile agent of another man, demeaning himself to satisfy the whims of a *toubab*?

These were the thoughts that ran through my mind as I watched Ndiak race to his doom for me.

My dear Aglaé, I have had only two or three true friends in my life. And Ndiak is, I am absolutely sure, the only one who sacrificed himself for me. I cannot be certain that, in similar circumstances, I would have done the same thing for him, because I do not believe that I have the same generosity of spirit.

XXIX

A few hours after Ndiak's departure, we too left the village of Ben, which is, as the crow flies, less than two leagues from the island of Gorée. To get there, we had to take dugouts from a small beach. It was a difficult task, navigating to Gorée from Anse Bernard: we needed a pilot to steer through the reefs that enclosed the beach, and when we arrived there none of the pilots who knew the way were still around.

I started to rejoice at this setback, which would give Ndiak more time to reach Nder and return. No doubt eager to rid himself of Maram, however, and to be paid handsomely by Estoupan de la Brüe for his loyalty, Seydou Gadio decided to commandeer a smaller dugout than the ones that were usually employed to connect the continent with the island of Gorée. So it was that Maram and Seydou left Anse Bernard aboard a dugout piloted by a young fisherman while I had to wait until the next morning before I could join them.

When I finally reached the island of Gorée, I rushed to the residence of M. de Saint-Jean, the island's governor and Estoupan de la Brüe's brother.

M. de Saint-Jean wore a neatly combed wig and his face was clean-shaven and powdered, while I was hairy and had not shaved for almost a week. I was dressed in the clothes that Maram had given me two days before: baggy white cotton trousers and a shirt with a blue, purple, and yellow pattern, open on the sides. Were it not for the fact that Ndiak had lent me a pair of camel-leather sandals, I would have been barefoot. Saint-Jean, on the other hand, was wearing a hat, a frock coat, breeches, silk stockings, and shoes with silver buckles. I had slept badly on the beach, under constant attack from mosquitoes, and despite the pagne with which I had protected my face, it was covered with red, swollen bites. Saint-Jean, standing on an interior balcony on the first floor of his official residence, looked surprised at my unseemly appearance.

Catching sight of his expression, I felt obligated to inform him that, due to a lack of time, I had not been able to recover my belongings, which had remained on the Anse Bernard beach. I begged his pardon at appearing before him in that state. Since I had not spoken French for several weeks, I expressed myself poorly. I was disconcerted by the strange rhythms of my native language and embarrassed by the Wolof accent I had acquired.

Saint-Jean, who had not removed his hat during the customary greetings that I had managed to reel off despite my confusion, asked me flat out what business I had that was so urgent I felt entitled to enter his home in such disarray. Without awaiting my answer, which he presumably already knew from Seydou Gadio, and since he was about to eat lunch, he invited me to share his meal. Following him into the dining room, which had a balcony overlooking the sea, I reflected that my physical appearance put me in a position of inferiority that risked harming Maram's cause.

I was all the more flustered since Saint-Jean looked to be at least twice my age. Much taller and more corpulent than me, he was as blond as his brother Estoupan de la Brüe was dark. His bulging pale blue eyes were the only distinguishing feature of his bland, flabby face, and they gave him an absent air that left me bewildered. He gestured vaguely with his left hand, in which he gripped an embroidered handkerchief, to my place at the table, facing his own. Upon his murmured command, a Black servant set the table for me. Without waiting, Saint-Jean began slurping down the soup he had been served. He tossed in two large pieces of bread, which he noisily sucked then swallowed without chewing. He did not look up at me until he had to demand that his wineglass be refilled.

Accompanying his question with a gesture as vague as the previous one, Saint-Jean asked me again in a voice drenched with irony: "So, Monsieur Adanson, to what do I owe the honor of your half-naked visit?"

When I had first landed in Gorée three years before, in the company of his brother, Saint-Jean had not acted disrespectfully toward me. No doubt the way in which Seydou Gadio had described my feelings for Maram had diminished me in his eyes, in tandem with my wretched appearance. The first time I had met him, I had been simply a dependable if little-known French scientist, worthy of respect from a patriotic standpoint; this time, I was merely a white man in African clothing. Saint-Jean was one of those men who are pitifully obsequious toward anyone they consider their superior, but pitiless when it comes to their inferiors, a rank to which I now found myself irrevocably relegated.

My pride, already ruffled by his impoliteness, could not

bear the condescending irony of his question. His demeaning tone backfired, giving me in a flash all the self-assurance I had misplaced. Since he had chosen to be rude, I decided to follow suit. In that sense, at least, we would be equals.

"Where is she?" I asked bluntly.

Not bothering to pretend he did not understand my meaning, Saint-Jean responded by banging the heel of his shoe against the floorboards.

"Under our feet."

"Maram is innocent. She did not commit the crime of which she has been accused."

"Ah, her name is Maram . . . But what crime are you referring to? If you mean the Black crushed to death by a giant boa, according to the reports I have received, it is of little interest to me. On the other hand, this woman knocked out my brother when he was about to honor her with a visit, as tradition dictates. You know perfectly well, Monsieur Adanson, that she is not innocent."

"Are you planning to send her back to Monsieur de la Brüe?"

"For one of her race, that woman is a Venus. My brother wasn't wrong about that—and nor were you, by the way. But she lost all appeal for him when she almost killed him. He has already told me that she is mine if I can find her. So I am selling her as a slave to the Americas."

Uttering this last sentence, Saint-Jean turned his face to the balcony with the sea view, and I realized that there must be a slave ship not far from the island. He intended to add Maram to its cargo.

His pale blue gaze alighted on me again and he went on: "I

am selling her to Monsieur de Vaudreuil, my friend the governor of Louisiana. He is fond of Black beauties, particularly the unruly ones. If you are fantasizing about buying her from me yourself, you should not be under any illusions: her price is far beyond your means. To amass enough money, you would have to mortgage your house in Paris, if you have one, and your parents' house too."

I thought I would die of rage, not so much because Saint-Jean was so openly contemptuous of my hereditary poverty, but because he imagined I would want to buy Maram. The idea horrified me. I had forgotten that the color of her skin, for men like him, relegated her to the status of a commodity in the great Atlantic slave trade. That oversight on my part had put me in the position of being brought back to the reality of a world I detested by a man I hated. Saint-Jean was trying to push me over the edge, and he succeeded magnificently when he rejected my final request. My throat tight, I asked him about the possibility of speaking to Maram.

"No, Monsieur Adanson, you will not be able to see her. The merchandise must not be given reasons to revolt. She must resign herself to her fate."

One of the servants must have filled my bowl with soup when I wasn't looking. I picked it up now and was about to throw it in Saint-Jean's face when I felt strong arms around my chest. His servant was crushing my arms to my sides so powerfully that I worried he would break the bones. Saint-Jean signaled to the man to release me and, rising from his seat, asked me coldly: "How could you fall in love with a Black woman? Is it because she let you screw her? Follow me—we're going to watch her leave."

X X X

I heard the telltale sounds of a rowboat approaching and the raised voices of sailors speaking French. As they rowed, they sang something like: "Pull, pull, cabin boy, I'll go from Lorient to Gorée. Pull, pull, cabin boy, then from Gorée to Saint-Domingue." The song was not quite as rudimentary as I am making it sound, but those were the words that struck me and that come to my memory as I write this.

I do not know why, but hearing that song, which should have been painful, was actually a moment of sweetness, as if the possibility that Maram, locked up in her cell, was able to hear it too, even if she did not understand the words, connected her to me forever. In that moment, she was still alive and, despite all the obstacles that Saint-Jean had placed between us, I still hoped to save her. Her voyage of no return to the land of slavery, as described in the words of the sailors' song, did not seem real to me. I loved Maram and I could not believe that she would be taken away from me, swallowed up by the horizon, devoured by America.

As Saint-Jean had suggested earlier when he banged his foot on the floor, Maram was a prisoner, along with other captured Africans, in cells located under the floor of the dining room. I was defeated by the governor of Gorée, and by his world—the strength of which, as inexorably powerful as the universal law of attraction, drew into its orbit the bodies and souls of Africans and Europeans alike.

Staggering, my spirit suddenly broken, I crossed the dining room to his suite, still escorted by his servant, and we walked down one of the two symmetrical, semicircular staircases that led to the house's inner courtyard. In the exact center of its façade, between the foot of those two staircases that led up to Saint-Jean's apartments, from where we had just come, was a heavy wooden hobnailed door. A guard standing nearby opened it on the governor's orders. A strong smell of urine made me flinch. All was dark. The guard went inside and I heard the sound of someone running. He opened another door, as heavy as the first, about twenty meters away, at the end of a corridor lined on both sides with doors through whose high, barred openings cells could be glimpsed. That second door overlooked the sea. A rush of fresh air carried the sickening stench from the cells toward us. The daylight that flooded the corridor, however, did not penetrate the interiors of the cells.

Covering his nose with a lace handkerchief, Saint-Jean went first through the corridor, walking—without a single sideways glance—toward the door at the other end. I followed him, seeking out Maram's eyes. All I saw were piles of shadows massed at the backs of the cells, far from the barred doors. Beyond the second door, a floating pier stretched out into the ocean. Saint-Jean stepped onto it. The sound of his footsteps on the wooden planks was drowned out by the vast murmur of the waves crashing onto the shiny black rocks that thrust jaggedly out of the sea. They looked like stone teeth, tensed to bite down on the water. I stood behind, at the edge of the pier, held still by the guard's hand on my shoulder.

The sailors—whose songs I had heard carried by the wind to Saint-Jean's dining room, one floor above—had tied their rowboat to the pier. Four of them, armed with muskets, approached Saint-Jean, who pointed at the cells. They advanced toward me and the guard made me step back into the corridor because the door was only wide enough for one person at a time to pass through it. Two sailors, muskets hanging from shoulder straps, entered the building without a word to me. They ordered the prison guard to open the first door and a dozen children, most of them naked, spilled out into the corridor. The biggest of them could not have been more than eight years old, while the youngest was perhaps four. They lined up two by two, holding hands, one of the sailors leading them and the other bringing up the rear. They came through the door. I saw them taking small steps forward, unsteady on their feet, probably blinded by the glimmers of sunlight reflecting off the surface of the sea. The sun was at its zenith and their shadows were hiding under their feet. When they reached the pontoon, they were grabbed by the armpits and lifted up as though they were no heavier than rag dolls, and it looked from where I stood as if they were simply tossed into the sea to drown, because the rowboat below, where they were caught by other sailors, was invisible beyond the last few planks of the jetty. Once they had all disappeared, swallowed up by the ocean, the guard opened the women's cell.

Maram was the first to emerge. She was dressed as she had been when I saw her leave the island of Gorée from the Anse

Bernard beach, as Seydou Gadio's prisoner. But now the strip of pale yellow cloth that she had worn as a headscarf the previous day was tied around her waist. I was almost level with her when she came out of the cell, her arms held out in front of her as the guard had ordered, so that he could more easily put her in chains. I could see her beautiful profile, the curve of her forehead, her nose with its contours accentuated by a beam of light that shone through the door open to the sea, to her left.

Saint-Jean had wanted me to see her one last time. While the idea that a Frenchman could fall in love with a Black woman did not compute with his conception of the world, he no doubt imagined that the bitterness of losing her to another man would make me suffer. But he did not suspect that what would drive me to the greatest depths of despair was seeing Maram hold out her hands toward the chains as if offering herself as a sacrifice, resigned to her fate.

Instinctively, and too fast this time for Saint-Jean's servant to stop me, I threw myself at the guard who was about to chain together Maram's wrists and knocked him to the ground. In the confusion that followed, I managed to grab one of Maram's hands and pull her toward the only open place within reach—the door that led to the pier. We ran through it, the two of us briefly together, side by side, her right hand in my left.

During the few seconds that our escape attempt lasted, I think I was happy. Better than any tender words or loving looks or passionate embraces, Maram's hot hand squeezing mine filled me with the sensation often described by those who claim to have died and been brought back to life. Instead of a rapid sequence of images from a life that was about to end, however, my mind gave me the dreamy mirage of a happy, imaginary life with her. A momentary intuition of intense joys as yet unexperienced. A symbiosis free of the disillusionment and resentment that this world, which hates difference, would no doubt have rained down upon our love.

Maram and I had gone through the door to a voyage of no return.

I pushed past two sailors as we fled and had almost reached the end of the pier when I heard a gunshot. It was written in the heavens that the bullet aimed at me would not hit its target. Carried forward by the momentum of our sprint, Maram did not collapse facedown at the end of the jetty, as I did, but fell into the water, grazing the prow of the rowboat filled with enslaved children. I saw her sink, then rise to the surface again, thrown upward into the air by a bubbling wave that carried her out to sea. She lay lifeless in a shroud of scarlet foam that was beginning to cover her entire body.

I was about to dive in after her, not to save her—it was already too late for that—but to join her in death. But before I could launch myself into the air I was tackled at the very edge of the pier. There, while I felt a knee pressed onto my back, I raised my neck and thought I saw, for one last time, Maram's luminous profile caught in a net of iridescent bubbles before being snatched away by the Atlantic. Ripples, little waves, then stillness.

XXXI

There was no humiliation that Saint-Jean, enraged at first by the loss of his "merchandise," did not try to inflict upon me. But none of them could touch me; I was alone in a world of suffering. Why had I shoved the guard, why had I grabbed Maram's hand? I was responsible for the death of the woman that I, so fleetingly, had loved. My actions had been reckless, selfish. I was just like Saint-Jean: a man who had wanted to possess her. Desperate to exonerate myself, I clung to the memory of her hand holding mine. Maram had seemed to accept the idea that we should run toward death together, that our fates should be one. But was that proof of love? Perhaps I was projecting onto this woman feelings that belonged only to me. She had given me her hand for a wedding march that had ended in a funeral march. My madness had sent her to hell; I was Orpheus to her Eurydice.

I was in thrall to so many paradoxical feelings, the prisoner of such bitter thoughts, that none of Saint-Jean's attempts to humiliate me had any effect. My mind was like one of those sea turtles that, if approached on a beach, will withdraw inside its shell, remaining there even if it is thrown onto a fire.

After all the slaves had been loaded onto the slave ship, I was locked in the women's cell, beneath Saint-Jean's dining room, beneath his feet. I found myself imprisoned in the darkness of that vile place where Maram had been a few hours before. Saint-Jean had been right: no other location in the world could have more cruelly rekindled my grief.

I felt ill; I was very hot. A sour stink of urine and excrement, no doubt left behind by all those terrified children, rose from the cell next door. I felt myself suffocating in the stench of inconsolable pain. Echoes of the screams of crazed women, of children torn from their mothers' arms, brothers mourning their sisters, the residue of all those silent suicides that soaked the dirt floor, seeped from the walls. I stood with my hands gripping the bars of my prison to stop myself from falling into the mire where my bare feet slid. Saint-Jean had made sure that the cell was not cleaned before locking me inside. Soon, I thought I could feel rats crawling over my feet and I began to weep at the idea that they had perhaps bitten Maram.

But the worst thing of all was that, alone in that cell, facing myself, I no longer recognized the man I had become. I had lost my reason. Why had I tried to save her in such a reckless way? Couldn't I have tried to delay her departure, to tempt Saint-Jean with promises that I would pay twice the amount he was being offered by M. de Vaudreuil? What would it have cost me to pretend that my passion for Maram was purely physical, to win Saint-Jean over with smutty jokes and manly solidarity? What did it matter *how* I did it if, at the end, Maram was still alive? But instead of keeping a cool head and exploiting the governor's baseness, I had let myself

be carried away on a wave of emotion upon seeing her hands
held out to be chained together.

I had interpreted her gesture as a sort of surrender, the
confession of a crime that she had not committed. Resigned
to the idea that she could never go home to the village of Sor,
convinced that her family's honor had been sullied forever
and that it was her fault, she had thought it only right to become a slave. But did she really know what awaited her on
the other side of the Atlantic? Did she think, like many other
slaves, that she was being taken to a slaughterhouse so that
white people could feed on her flesh? Was she indifferent to
thoughts of her death, so far from home? I knew very well
what awaited her in the sugarcane fields of Saint-Domingue
or in the bed belonging to M. de Vaudreuil.

Saint-Jean kept me in that cell only half a day. He did not
release me out of pity but because he knew it was not in his
interest to keep me there longer. I had an advantage over him
that would prevent him reporting my love-crazed attempt to
save a Black slave to the French authorities: there was a very
high risk that I would denounce him to his superiors. Selling beautiful slave girls for his own profit would probably
not have led to his dismissal, because it was a practice tolerated among governors of the island of Gorée as long as they
remained discreet about it. But it could have harmed his career prospects. It would not have been wise to hand over to
his competitors—men who were eyeing the same prestigious
posts as he was—a witness to his personal enrichment at the
expense of the Senegal Concession. However minimal the
losses to his revenue, one could not, at that time, steal with
impunity from the king of France.

Saint-Jean must have been kicking himself for saying too much to me about his sale of Maram to M. de Vaudreuil. I understood this from the letter he had delivered to me after my release. He wrote that I had not behaved as a reasonable man, and that my academic career would not be well served by publicizing my misguided passion for an African. As for himself, he considered himself sufficiently avenged for the loss of income I had occasioned him by the four hours I had spent in that cell, and which he regretted having had to inflict upon me. But it had been his duty to lock me up to save face with all his subordinates, who expected no less from a man of his authority. He concluded that we were even if I would consent to write, upon my return to France, something about the good governance of Gorée. By "good governance," he meant the revenues he was procuring for the Senegal Concession through the trade in slaves that he succeeded in bringing to and sending from the island. About four hundred souls every year, at the period when I was in Senegal.

Thus it was that I found myself freed before I had had time to ponder my own miserable fate. If I had spent longer locked in that cell where Maram had been before me, my grief would have been mixed with the difficulty of explaining to my parents that I had ruined my future career for the love of a Black woman. Whatever affection he felt for me, my father would not have accepted this, and I am not certain that my mother would have forgiven me either.

Saint-Jean ordered me to leave Gorée and to return to Saint-Louis by the quickest route, along the coastline. I agreed, since this was the path that Ndiak would have to take to return from Nder, where he had gone to plead Maram's cause with his father, the king of Waalo.

When I landed on the continent, I found my armed escort and my porters waiting for me on the beach. Nobody knew—or at least nobody wanted to tell me—where Seydou Gadio had gone, and this was also true for the whereabouts of my horse, which had disappeared at the same time as the old warrior. They wouldn't meet my gaze. No doubt they thought I looked strangely dirty, scruffy and wild-eyed, but they did not mock me, perhaps sensing that I was so wretched that I wanted to die.

Indifferent to my own appearance, I told them to lead me to the village of Yoff, on the coastline. Without Ndiak and Seydou Gadio, there were only eight of us. I followed the seven men from a distance, while they walked as slowly as possible to let me catch up. Through the Krampsanè Forest, I walked as if weighed down by remorse, dragging my feet and stopping frequently. As soon as I spotted an ebony tree lost amid all the palm trees and date palms, I knelt down and palpated the earth at its base. Perhaps it was on this exposed root that Maram, exhausted, had rested her head while awaiting death after her escape from Estoupan de la Brüe's ship? Perhaps it was there that she had buried the red leather staff embedded with cowries that the old healer Ma-Anta had given to her? Fragments of Maram's story flooded my memory, and an imaginary geography replaced the real one of my surroundings. I went from ebony tree to ebony tree, following the trail of Maram's narrative rather than the path to Yoff.

When we finally got there, after a day of wandering, I was welcomed by the chief of the village of Yoff, whose acquaintance I had made during my first trip to Cap Vert. Saliou Ndoye, like everyone else who had seen me in that state, seemed horrified by my appearance. I realized that, if I wanted to be left alone to grieve, I would have to put a brave face on it. So I took off the clothes that I had been wearing since Maram gave them to me, although I did still have the presence of mind to have them carefully cleaned before they were stored in one of my trunks. I washed, shaved, and changed. I acted as if I had become one of Vaucanson's automata, the servant of my body's machine, with my will seeming to play no part. My host, Saliou Ndoye, was the first to realize—having known the Michel Adanson of before: naïve, curious, sociable, quite cheerful—that the young man standing before him now was no longer the same person. I had become almost aphasic, apathetic. Nothing interested me anymore, not even the rare plants or other curiosities of nature to be found in the bush around Yoff. I could no longer bear to look at the sea: I hated it because it had taken Maram away from me. Indeed, my antipathy was so intense that I wondered how I would ever make it back to France on a ship. The seasickness from which I had always suffered would be nothing compared with the melancholia that had overwhelmed me and that would, I hoped, diminish once I was home again. I missed the cold, the smell of damp undergrowth and mushrooms, the sound of bells punctuating life in the fields and cities of my country.

The human race in its entirety struck me now as detestable, and I hated myself most of all. An unceasing rage now darkened my view of the world, and, with that wisdom common among the Senegalese, Saliou Ndoye did not take offense at my rudeness, which was, he believed, involuntary. He left me in peace in the enclosure he had assigned to me and my escort.

Over the course of three nights, I slowly pulled myself together. On the morning of the fourth day we left Yoff by the coastal path along the beach that would lead us straight to Saint-Louis, to the north. I reproached myself for not leaving earlier, because, in my selfishness, I had forgotten that I was forcing Ndiak to ride farther to reach us than would have been necessary had I covered more of that distance myself.

And, just as I had imagined, two days after leaving Yoff, I spotted him on the beach: a tiny, far-off figure, advancing toward us.

He was on foot, not on horseback, but his tall, frail outline was unmistakable. Since the time I first saw him he had grown quickly in height, but he had not filled out. His blue tunic floated around him like a small sail swollen by the wind, pulling him along in its whirls and gusts, sometimes forward, sometimes backward. He was walking with difficulty, his swaying, obstinate gait slowed down by a very bulky brown-colored object that he held in his long, thin arms against his chest. I started to run toward him and soon I could see him clearly. He was in a pitiful state, his clothes filthy, his yellow Morocco-leather riding boots—of which he was so proud—covered with large brownish stains. What he was carrying in his arms, the way a father might carry a sleeping child, was the English saddle given to him by the king of Kayor at the village of Meckhé.

We stood there facing each other in silence, Ndiak and I, easily guessing from the look on each other's faces the sadness of our mutual stories.

We had come across each other near the village of Keur Damel. The remains of a few fences were lying on the beach, carried there by the wind. I ordered a large mat to be laid on the ground and the two of us sat there, with our backs to the sea. Ndiak had not eaten since the previous day, and, while he sucked the end of a sugarcane to give himself enough strength to listen to me, I told him about Maram's death in Gorée. His eyes were filled with tears by the end of my account, and we sat there silently until Ndiak spoke these words that I have not forgotten:

"Life is very strange. Barely seven days ago, this village of Keur Damel was, for us, a place of no significance. Today it is the source of all our sorrows. The man who advances along the path of life will come upon junctions, fateful crossroads that he will not recognize as such until after he has passed them. Keur Damel was the intersection of all possible paths to our destinies. If Seydou Gadio and I had chosen, Adanson, to have you transported on that stretcher to Yoff rather than the village of Ben, either you would be dead or someone other than Maram would have brought you back to life just as she did. During your convalescence in Yoff, Baba Seck, who would have arrived before us in Ben, would perhaps have been killed by Maram's giant snake. If she'd had time to get rid of her uncle's body in a distant corner of the Krampsanè Forest, or even under the land of her enclosure, nobody in Ben would ever have known her true identity. Seydou Gadio would not have found his musket. Maram would still be alive and I would not have gone to Nder to vainly beg my father, the heartless king, to pardon her."

When I heard Ndiak's last words, I could not help weeping in turn.

Behind us we could hear the jingling of millions of little shells shuffled by the ebb and flow of the tide. Fragments of speech from the men in our escort, who for the sake of discretion were standing quite far away from us, came to us in ripples of sound whirling in the sea wind that blew sand all around us.

After a long moment spent in a reverie sparked by what Ndiak had said to me about the hazards of fate, I asked him where his horse was. Had it been stolen from him, as mine had been? Ndiak told me that it had collapsed while running that very morning, after galloping almost without respite since they had left the village of Ben and headed to Nder. When Mapenda Fall had sunk suddenly to its death, Ndiak had been thrown onto the sandy beach, which had softened the blow of his fall. It had been a terrible struggle to free his saddle. To unbuckle it, he'd been forced to disembowel the poor animal, hence the dried bloodstains on his boots.

I knew how fond Ndiak had been of that horse, which he had named after his mother, and I was surprised by the detached tone in which he recounted its sad end.

"I will not weep for that horse," he added, "just as I will not miss the world from which I come. When I asked my father to pardon Maram, he replied that it was none of his business and that, if I was so fond of her, all I had to do was buy her from Estoupan de la Brüe. Oh, our discussion did not last long: the word of the king of Waalo is irrevocable. And since all the riches I had in the world were my horse and my saddle, I thought I could sell them both at a good price once I returned to Cap Vert, so that you could buy Maram's freedom. I lost the horse, but I still have the saddle from the king of Kayor. I have been carrying it for too long. It will be of no more use to me now. It is yours, Adanson."

Ndiak had said this in a serene voice. He was not joking; his eyes were not blinking as they did when he wished to make mischief with me. He was smiling at the new life he saw for himself.

"My horse died trying to save a young woman from slavery," he added. "And it had a good end. What price did the king of Kayor pay for it from Whites or Moors? The price of ten slaves? I should never have lent my mother's name to that gift horse, which should have filled me with shame instead of exciting my pride. I realized that just after seeing my father. So I have decided to leave the kingdom of Waalo for the kingdom of Kayor. The only person who knows this yet, apart from you, Adanson, is my mother. She gave me her blessing. But I will not go to Mboul or Meckhé to add one more useless mouth to the court of the king of Kayor. I will go to Pir Gourèye instead. There, I will study the holy book of the Qur'an so that I can try to attain wisdom. It is the only place in this country where it is forbidden to buy or sell slaves. In Pir Gourèye, a horse does not come at the cost of the freedom of young men or young women like Maram. I hope that the great marabout will allow me to become one of his disciples."

After speaking these words, Ndiak took off his boots and plunged his right hand into the immaculate sand of the beach. He picked up a handful and rubbed it over his face, his hands, and his feet to wash them, then he got to his feet. With his head lowered to the ground and the palms of his hands turned up to the sky, he prayed to his god for a long time while dusk reddened the sky behind him.

XXXII

By the next morning, Ndiak was no longer there. At the spot
on the beach where he and I had reunited, an encampment
had been set up by my people. We had shared a last meal in
the slowly dying firelight while he tried to console me. Then,
at dawn, he had slipped away while I was still sleeping without bidding me farewell. He had headed east, his back to the
Atlantic, one of our porters told me. Presumably he was going
to Pir Gourèye, as he had said.

His absence hurt me as much as Maram's. It felt to me as
if Ndiak had died too. Now, in my mind, the two of them
traveled through unreal, dreamlike worlds, at the intersection
of paths that seemed to take them ever farther away from me.

My head felt empty; nothing interested me anymore. I no
longer observed the plants or birds or shells that I could have
collected along the beach that I followed toward Saint-Louis.
I realized how a place, no matter how beautiful and interesting
it might be in and of itself, ceases to mean anything when it is
no longer populated with our dreams, hopes, and aspirations.
From that point on, the sight of baobab, ebony, and palm
trees only rekindled my desire to see oaks, beeches, poplars,
and birches. Nothing in Africa was to my taste anymore. I

was tired of the stark light of its shadow-devouring sun. Everything I had thought beautiful, new, extraordinary upon my arrival in Senegal—people, fruit, plants, strange animals, insects, reptiles—had lost its wondrousness for me. I missed the coolness of morning mists, the smell of mushrooms in the undergrowth, the sound of our mountain waterfalls. My only dream now was to return to France.

Once I was back at the island of Saint-Louis, I hardly ever went outdoors. Estoupan de la Brüe did not ask to meet me. No doubt his brother had written to him describing what had happened at the village of Ben and the island of Gorée, and he had no desire to hear me talk about Maram. Instead of writing him a report on the mission he had assigned me, I simply sent him the English saddle that Ndiak had left behind. I accompanied this with a short note explaining that the saddle was a gift from the king of Kayor that suggested he was on good terms with the English as well as with the French. I do not know what Estoupan de la Brüe did with that information but, five years after my departure from Senegal, the English took possession of Saint-Louis and Gorée.

Estoupan de la Brüe, as eager for me to return to France as I was, provided me with a little garden very close to the fort of Saint-Louis. Soon my only amusement came when I was in that garden, attempting to acclimatize plants and fruit from France, the seeds of which had been sent to me by the Jussieu brothers, my masters at the Royal Academy of Sciences in Paris. And it was through that little French garden that homesickness imperceptibly replaced my grief over the losses of Maram and Ndiak.

After briefly abandoning the description of plants in favor of relationships with humans, I now returned to my first passion, and little by little I rediscovered my love for the study of nature. I gradually picked up my old working habits and launched myself into botanical research with an ardor that grew ever stronger because it enabled me to forget the recent tragedy. It was during this period that I conceived my project for a universal encyclopedia, and that I devoted all my intelligence to this end, day and night.

Sometimes, despite my new preoccupations, a sort of black melancholy would sweep down on me again. It would suddenly fill my mind and the only way I could rid myself of it was to concentrate on my senses. Once I had identified the sensorial impression that had reminded me of Maram, I would try desperately to eradicate it and, if that proved impossible, to ignore it.

Five weeks before my return to France, I undertook one last trip in a dugout canoe on the Senegal River to the village of Podor, where the Concession had a trading post. I had given myself the task of mapping the river's meanders and collecting the seeds of several rare plants that I would send back to the Jardin du Roi. I would often ask the *laptots*—fishermen who acted as interpreters for the French—who piloted our trading canoe to drop me off in different places so that I could make topographic measurements, or collect plants and hunt animals. I was absorbed by the descriptions, which I wished to be precise and which I accompanied with sketches, imagining that I could turn them into engravings for my encyclopedia, my "Universal Orb." Larger animals such as hippopotamuses or those manatees that European sailors had once mistaken for sirens were abundant in that part of the river, far from Saint-Louis.

Midway through the voyage, nothing of any note had happened to me. And since our trading canoe could barely make any headway along the river due to the strong cross-currents, I decided that rather than merely moping around, I would spend most of my time on the left bank of the Senegal River. Accompanied by a *laptot*, I distracted myself by hunting every animal I could find. Nor did I neglect to pick the strangest flowers I spotted and to prepare them for my herbaria. Absorbed by these activities, I managed not to think about Maram anymore until, late one afternoon, she suddenly reappeared in my mind with a sharpness that troubled me.

Knowing that there is nothing immaterial in our thoughts and that they are often the result of strong impressions upon one or several of our senses, I immediately sought out whatever it was that might have caused Maram to emerge from my memory. I quickly realized that it had not been the sight of an animal or even of a plant in this part of the bush, almost identical to the vegetation around the village of Sor, that had brought about this return of my suffering, but the smell of burning eucalyptus bark. When Maram told me her story, in the dimness of her hut in Ben, the incense smoke that rose from a small terra-cotta vessel decorated with openwork figures had smelled of burned eucalyptus bark. At this memory, I was overcome with such sadness and dizziness that I fell to the ground. And there, on my knees, despite the *laptot*'s presence, I began to sob violently, harder than I had ever wept before, even in the immediate aftermath of Maram's death on the island of Gorée.

So I was still at the mercy of any sensation that brought Maram to mind! I realized that the memory of her would not cease tormenting me until I had left Senegal. But where I knelt at that moment, on a riverbank in the middle of nowhere, far from Saint-Louis, I was caught in the trap of my regrets, for my love severed at the root, for all my shattered hopes. And when I considered the cruel truth that it would have been impossible for me and Maram to live together because of the prejudices in our respective worlds, and that even if she had still been alive we could not have been united in the eyes of God or of men, my tears ran dry and I was filled with an immense rage.

In that moment my anger was greater than my reason, and, desperate to get rid of the smell of burning eucalyptus, I could find no other solution than starting a huge bushfire in which it would be lost, overpowered by the odors of thousands of other burning trees, herbs, and flowers.

Since the practice of burning crops to fertilize the soil was common in Senegal, the *laptot* who was with me—although a fisherman rather than a farmer—was not surprised to see me starting a gigantic blaze. With his help, I think I set fire to several hectares of bush.

The suffocating heat of the late afternoon was intensified by the flames rising around us, and we were both pouring with sweat. So it was that, pursued at last by our own fire, on the verge of exhaustion, we had to take refuge on the riverbank, where we had just enough time to clamber into our dugout. Barely had we moved away from the bank when we saw some long tree trunks with dark, cracked bark moving toward us through the water. They were black crocodiles, a common sight in those parts, come to collect the tribute of grilled flesh offered to them by the burning bush. And I could see now, fleeing the blaze, animals of all sizes and colors diving into the Senegal, where they floundered—half-burned, half-drowned—before being caught in the enormous pink or pale yellow mouths of the black crocodiles.

As night fell, my *laptot* companions and I—floating in our dugout, not far from the scene of that massacre—watched in silence as the blaze battled the water. Flames swallowed trees that fell into the river, the water steaming from all those sacrifices of wood and flesh, sap and blood, that I had offered it. But in this chaos of blinding lights and acrid smoke, in this apocalypse of water, fire, and scorching air, despite all the energy I had spent to eradicate it, I thought I could still smell the heady scent of burned eucalyptus that reminded me ceaselessly of Maram. Maram, always Maram.

XXXIII

Back in Saint-Louis after my river voyage to the village of Podor, where I had spent only three days before growing weary of it, I began to put all my affairs in order in preparation for my return to France. I had to classify and pack into crates the collections of shells, plants, and seeds that I had put together in Senegal during the previous four years. That activity occupied my mind for a whole month, keeping the memory of Maram more or less at bay. But the day before my departure from Senegal, on the evening when I began sorting through my personal belongings, I thought that my heart, caught by the inferno I had started on the river, was about to be reduced to ashes.

In one of my trunks full of clothing, I found—on top of the pile, washed and neatly folded, as I had asked my servants to do with them—the white cotton trousers and the shirt decorated with purple crabs and yellow and blue fish that Maram had given me to change into on that fatal night in her hut. Even though they still smelled of shea butter—not a scent I had ever liked—I decided to keep them. I would never put them on again in my life, but those clothes were one of very few tangible proofs that Maram had cared about me, that she had wanted to take care of me. On the other hand, I threw away the shirt, stockings, and breeches soiled by my fever sweats in Keur Damel. Those clothes were covered with reddish stains that the dust-filled rainstorm had spread over them after I had washed them and hung them to dry on a fence in Maram's enclosure. In the candlelight that illuminated my bedroom in the fort of Saint-Louis, they looked for all the world like dried bloodstains.

One by one I placed my clothes on the floor to decide what to keep and what to leave behind. But when I was close to reaching the bottom of the trunk, which the candlelight could not penetrate, I felt something under my fingertips that did not have the texture of clothing. Thinking I had touched one of those large, harmless lizards known in Senegal as geckos, I hurriedly withdrew my hand. But how could a gecko have gotten into my second trunk of clothing, which had not been opened since I was at the village of Yoff in Cap Vert, several months before? I raised my candle and discovered that the skin I had touched really did belong to a reptile, but not to a gecko, as I had at first thought. In the dancing light of the little flame, I felt faint with mingled joy and fear as I saw— neatly folded, black with pale yellow stripes, as shiny as if it still covered the body of a living animal—the skin of Maram's snake-totem.

Now I understood why I had smelled shea butter when I opened my trunk: Maram had used that natural ointment to keep the snakeskin from drying out and losing its colors. It was probably also a ritual that she performed daily to propitiate her *rab*. But how had this boa skin ended up in my trunk?

Had Maram put it there? Even if she had been able to gain access to my trunk, however, why would she have done that?

My throat was tight. I felt certain that, no matter how it had ended up in my belongings, that snakeskin could be the decisive proof—even more than the trusting hand she had slipped into mine when I pulled her toward death on the jetty in Gorée—of Maram's love for me. And my heart contracted at the thought that all the happy lifetimes I had shared with her in dreams since her death had gained a new layer of reciprocity that made them more precious to me than ever. So Maram had loved me! Had she started to have feelings for me long before my desperate attempt to save her on the jetty? Could it have begun when I told her I had come from Saint-Louis to the village of Ben because I was curious about her? Was it because I had listened to her story almost without interruption? A new ocean of sweet ideas opened up before me and I would almost have felt happy had not this surprising evidence of Maram's feelings toward me not been connected in my mind with the cruel awareness of her death.

Soon, I was fully focused on working out how the skin of her protective *rab* had been placed inside my trunk. I ruled out the idea that Maram herself had put it there because she was constantly guarded by Seydou Gadio. Nor did I think it could have been Senghane Faye, her messenger, the only villager in Ben who had tried to defend her when Seydou had announced that he was taking her as his prisoner to Gorée. Senghane would not have had an opportunity to do it, because my escort, as well as Ndiak, had kept a careful watch over my belongings.

The beginning of an answer to that mystery came to

222 · DAVID DIOP

mind when I remembered how Seydou Gadio had claimed to have found Maram's tracks in the bush. If it were true, as the warrior had said, that she had deliberately dragged a staff along the ground, allowing him to find her under that ebony tree, and if it were also true that Seydou, despite his uncompromising nature, had given Maram time to bury the old healer's staff, wasn't it also plausible that they had struck another bargain, born from the warrior's fear of upsetting such a powerful woman? It would hardly have been surprising if Seydou, having been promised that she would not try to escape, and above all out of fear of the mystical reprisals in which he believed, had agreed to Maram's request that he hide the totem in my trunk. In hindsight it seemed to me that the warrior had only been so determined to take her to Gorée because Maram had commanded him to do so. His anger with me was due to his fear of the young woman who knew how to train boas to kill men. Seydou was the sole member of my entourage who could have had access to my trunk without raising suspicion.

The next morning, I asked the guards at the fort for news of Seydou Gadio. I wanted to know if it had been he who had hidden the snakeskin in my trunk at Maram's request. I also hoped he would recount to me Maram's exact words. I was in a rush, because I had to leave for France the next day, but the guards told me Seydou had not returned to Saint-Louis in a long time and that even his acolyte, Ngagne Bass, did not know where he was.

So, whether because he feared that I would ask him why he had insisted on taking Maram as a prisoner to Gorée, or because he thought I would demand the return of the horse

he stole from me, Seydou Gadio, the old warrior, had not returned to the island of Saint-Louis. Perhaps he had gone directly back to Nder, since his mission had been to watch over
Ndiak and myself for the king of Waalo rather than serve
the director of the Senegal Concession. While I was almost
certain that Seydou, who was Waalo-Waalo, had taken the
same path I had taken along the beach after leaving Cap
Vert, it was possible that he had turned northeast, toward
Nder, without bothering to inform Estoupan de la Brüe of
my misadventures. After thinking it over, I decided I was glad
not to have seen him again, because I would probably have
found it unbearable to hear Maram's last message for me,
whatever it might have been, repeated by Seydou Gadio.

Estoupan gave me a cold reception when I went to take
my leave of him, a few hours before my departure for France.
The French language has the advantage of allowing one to
formally discharge one's duties of politeness without putting
one's heart into it but also without causing offense. So it was
that, in a tone as civilized and cold as his own, I reported the
success of my plantings in the little garden that he had provided for me at the end of my stay. The fruit and vegetables of
Europe that had had time to grow there in profusion demonstrated that the lands near the Senegal River were favorable to
all forms of cultivation. If I'd had the time and the desire, and
above all if he had encouraged me with his open-mindedness,
I would have followed up this agricultural report with the
recommendation that the thousands of Africans sent by the
Senegal Concession to the Americas would have been better
employed cultivating arable land in Africa. Sugarcane grew
easily in Senegal and it would have been less costly for France

224 · DAVID DIOP

to import the sugar it needed so badly from West Africa than from the Antilles. But Estoupan de la Brüe was the last person likely to be receptive to this handsome speech, which I barely suggested in the account of my voyage that I published four years after my return to Paris. The truth is, my idea was incompatible with the wealth of a world that had revolved around the buying and selling of millions of Black people for more than a century. We would have to carry on eating sugar impregnated with their blood. The Africans had not been wrong to believe—and perhaps they still believe this now—that we were deporting them to the Americas so we could eat them like livestock.

XXXIV

I left Senegal for France without regret in late 1753. And when I arrived at the port in Brest on January 4, 1754, it was so cold that all the shrubs—and even the seeds that I was planning to donate to the Jardin du Roi—had frozen. A parrot with yellow and green feathers, which I had thought I might acclimatize to life in Paris, also died. My heart was frozen too; I was no longer the same person I had been before I left. My father had died only a few months earlier, and my sadness was increased by the knowledge that I could never have explained to him, any more than I could to my mother, the reason for my profound melancholy.

I had no one in whom to confide, and my family and friends ascribed my state of mind to the fatigue of an African voyage. For want of anything better to do with my life, I ended up compressing my grief so tightly within my heart, devoting all my energy to the quest of inventing a universal method of classification for all beings, that I thought I had made it vanish from my life forever.

Like all young people—or so I suppose—I gradually blocked out the heartache I felt for Maram. In truth, my passion for botany had once again taken possession of me, and I noticed that in the rare moments when my mind was empty, particularly at night, just before falling asleep, the image of Maram would appear there less and less often. Sometimes, overcome with remorse, I would open my trunk of Senegalese treasures to touch the skin of her totem. I did not look after it as I should have, and I could see that, as it dried out, it lost the luster of its two dazzling colors, that jet black and that pale yellow, similar to the hollow of a calabash. But, little by little, the snakeskin ceased to evoke Maram. Neither the woman I loved nor her totem seemed able to acclimatize to Paris and its prevailing spirit of rationalism.

Certain memories wither, like a delicate plant losing its leaves, when the mind that feeds them no longer tends them with the same affection, the same solicitude as before. This is probably because it is absorbed by the aspirations of a very different world, too far removed from the rituals of the one left behind. Since I no longer had a reason to speak Wolof, I eventually stopped dreaming in that language a few months after my return from Senegal. And, as if the two were connected, the more that the language I shared with Maram slipped from my mind, the less she appeared in my memories and dreams.

My first betrayal was offering the skin of Maram's totem as a gift to the Duke of Ayen, Louis de Noailles, to whom I also dedicated my *Voyage to Senegal*, published in 1757. I think he liked that spectacular present more than he liked my book. I heard that he would take the boa skin from the cabinet of curiosities where he kept it and amuse himself by unfolding its entire, enormous length in the dining room of his mansion to spoil his guests' appetites. He called it "Michel Adanson's skin," and, since I had remained vague when telling him how it had come into my possession, he naturally claimed that I was the one who had killed that gigantic snake. But he did point out that, given its size, I could not possibly have managed the feat without the aid of ten Black hunters experienced in the pursuit of those monsters, such as only Africa can produce.

I am not proud to admit this now, but time gradually erased Maram's face from my memory and I ended up assimilating my passion for her into a romantic adventure that I hid away out of shame, a youthful folly without consequence. My ambition as a scientist grew so all-consuming that I sacrificed Maram to it without remorse. And, a prisoner of my quest for fame and glory, considered by my peers to be a specialist on anything related to Senegal, I published a pamphlet for the Bureau of Colonies extolling the advantages of the slave trade for the Senegal Concession in Gorée.

I argued in favor of that vile traffic, lining up figures in support of it and going against my own convictions, which I kept closely hidden, buried deep in my soul. Lost in the study of plants, led by the hope of one day achieving personal glory by publishing my "Universal Orb," I gradually abandoned my principles and lost sight of Maram—and, with her, the tangible reality of slavery. Or at least I hid that reality from my own eyes behind an abstract, logical demonstration of its financial advantages. From my present vantage point, I may say that I killed Maram a second time when I wrote that pamphlet praising the slave trade in Gorée.

My father had agreed to my choice not to follow a religious calling only on the condition that I should succeed in becoming a member of the Académie. I substituted one priesthood for another and, like a profane clergyman, devoted myself to botany, body and soul. A voluntary prisoner of a sworn oath, I found the strength one day to write against the love I had begun to feel for a young woman almost at the very moment when I lost her forever.

It was not until more than fifty years after Maram's death that an event took place—an event I will describe to you a little later in these notebooks, Aglaé—that revived in me extremely painful memories of the profound love I had never stopped feeling for her, despite my mind's long, willful forgetting.

When I married your mother, my dear Aglaé, Maram no longer existed in my mind. Jeanne was much younger than I, and I must say that in the early years of our marriage, she brought me back to life. I opened my heart to her love of theater, poetry, opera. Almost a year before your birth, your mother even managed to drag me away from my desk. She took me to the Théâtre du Palais-Royal for the opening night of Gluck's *Orpheus and Eurydice* on August 2, 1774, to be precise.

At that point, I was still trying to reconcile my love for your mother with my academic ambitions. In 1770, it was her energy that helped me overcome the disappointment of seeing the position that had been promised to me at the Jardin du Roi assigned to a plagiarist, a botanical impostor who happened to be the nephew of my former mentor Bernard de Jussieu. It was your mother, again, who made a success of the natural history classes I gave in our home on rue Neuve-des-Petits-Champs for two consecutive years, from 1772 to 1773. She has a talent for social relations that I sadly lack. Your mother realized long before I did that I would have no chance of publishing my "Universal Orb" without the support of powerful people at the Court. Her social skills and her connections would have borne fruit, and Fortune would have smiled upon me, had I not turned away from that influential lady every time your mother brought me into her presence.

On that night in August 1774, I felt happy that your mother had taken me to the opera. We had excellent seats, in the Duke of Ayen's box. One would not have to be especially perceptive to guess that this patron of the arts and sciences, to whom I had dedicated my *Voyage to Senegal* and given Maram's giant boa skin, had come to my botanical lessons only because he was attracted to your mother. Wishing to be agreeable to her, and knowing her tastes in music, Louis de Noailles had lent us his box at the Théâtre du Palais-Royal.

We arrived late, for a reason I have forgotten, though I am sure it was my fault. Down in the pit, the orchestra had just finished tuning up. By the time we reached our seats, the crowd had fallen silent. Opera glasses were turned in our direction. The cream of Paris was there, and I felt ill at ease in their company. I sat back in my seat while your mother, her bosom thrust forward, was the only one of us visible from the neighboring boxes. I remember her face illuminated by the thousands of candles in the chandelier suspended above the stage, where the set for the first act was already in place: a copse of trees, painted on canvas, and, below this, a marble gravestone fashioned from cardboard. A small troop of shepherds and shepherdesses dropped fresh flowers on Eurydice's grave. Then, while the choir lamented, Orpheus appeared, weeping over the death of his beloved.

Submerged by the poignant songs that rose from the

stage, swept along by Gluck's sublime music, your mother's face, which would turn toward me now and then, reflected the characters' emotions. In truth, it was less the reflections of their emotions than a series of expressions from deep within her, as if Eurydice, then Orpheus, took over her whole being, possessing her soul, shining from her eyes.

Eros, touched by Orpheus's lamentations, asked Jupiter, the god of gods, to let the prince of Thrace enter the underworld to search for his Eurydice. Jupiter thundered his agreement, but only on the impossible condition that Orpheus did not turn around to look at Eurydice during their journey back to life.

Orpheus descends to hell and takes Eurydice's hand. The soft accents of a flute rise airily over a backdrop of violins. But Eurydice refuses to follow Orpheus, because he will not meet her eyes. She does not understand how the man she loved won't even look at her after such a long separation. Does Orpheus still love her? Is he afraid that death has disfigured her? Eurydice, in tears, withdraws her hand from Orpheus's. "But my hand by yours is no longer held tight! / Why do you flee my eyes which you once loved so?" Poor Eurydice knows nothing of the terrible condition that Jupiter has imposed on Orpheus. Pained by his beloved's fears, disobeying Jupiter's impossible order, Orpheus turns to Eurydice to prove to her that he still loves her. She vanishes instantly, a shade taken back by Hades. A clamor of violins. Wails from the choir. Orpheus in despair.

Orpheus exhorts himself to commit suicide, his only chance of being with Eurydice for eternity. But while, in the myth, Orpheus does end up killing himself so that he can rejoin his beloved in the underworld, Gluck has other ideas.

And in a final bouquet of soft violins and tender flute, the god Love saves Orpheus from death by bringing Eurydice back to life.

During the three acts of that opera, I saw your mother weep, sometimes from sadness and sometimes from joy, and I do not think I will ever forget her tearful smile the sole time she turned her face fully toward me. I took her right hand in my left and I squeezed it quite hard.

XXXV

Time passed. Your mother and I separated. If any proof remains that we once loved each other, it is you, Aglaé. You are named after Aphrodite's messenger, the youngest of the Three Charites, radiant with beauty. You owe your name to your mother, whose predilection for the Greeks' wonderful fables I always admired, even if I did not share it for long. I could have been happy with the two of you had not botany deprived me of the time my love for you needed. That science was my tyrannical mistress. She burned everything around me, and I could not tear myself away from her despite her all-consuming jealousy.

It is only since I began writing these notebooks for you, Aglaé, that I think I have managed to fully free myself from her grip. But, in truth, I did not start to liberate myself from my obsession with publishing my universal encyclopedia until April of last year, just after the failure of my final attempt to publish all of its one hundred and twenty volumes.

I wrote the emperor another letter, in which I asked him to become the patron of my "Universal Orb." His reply, with its promise of three thousand francs, seemed like an act of charity. Alms for the last whim of an old Académie member. I thought about refusing it, because I was not asking for an additional pension. I confided my decision to my friend Claude-François Le Joyand, who urged me to accept this imperial favor. If I refused it, he would be in an awkward position, because it had been he who had used his connections to convince the emperor to even glance at my letter. "One good deed can lead to another," he kept repeating. "In the end, the emperor will understand the usefulness of your encyclopedia for France's scientific standing in Europe."

It was with these words that Le Joyand welcomed me into his home on April 4, 1805. I had accepted his invitation so that he could console me once again for my umpteenth editorial setback. Claude-François Le Joyand was one of the very few of my Académie colleagues whom I also considered my friend. But I was extremely disappointed when, in the entrance hall of his apartment, I found quite a large number of people, some of whom were already known to me. Guettard, my worst enemy, was there. Lamarck too. I had believed, wrongly, that I was the only guest. Le Joyand was maneuvering to become the assistant director for the perpetual secretariat of Class II of the new Imperial Institute of the Sciences and the Arts, and to win support he was playing the role of mediator between the old and the new academic worlds.

After introducing me to a dozen people whom he had, in his own words, gathered in my honor, he took me by the arm and led me to a double-leaf door which opened into a large reception room. The others followed us inside, including Guettard and Lamarck, who had greeted me politely, almost cordially, with none of the veiled irony I had been expecting. But I had taken no more than a few steps inside that room when I suddenly froze.

Seeing me turn pale, interrupting the compliments paid to me by a woman at whom I was not looking, Le Joyand introduced the person whose appearance had so violently caught my attention. Seeing her, I thought I could feel my heart curl in on itself. And, while he told me how he had made an agreement with her owner so that she could be brought to his salon, I hardly listened to a word he said because it seemed to me that, having returned from the depths of hell where I had abandoned her so long ago, Maram was staring at me, with sadness in her eyes.

It was a painting. A large portrait of a Black woman, in a white dress and headscarf, sitting on a chair draped with blue velvet, one breast bared, her head turned three-quarters toward me. Le Joyand had hung it opposite the entrance to his reception room. I had not spotted it at first, because I had been too busy greeting the other guests. I had seen it only when I raised my eyes to examine the place where he was leading me.

Pleased with himself, Le Joyand thought he had succeeded in transporting me to a period that he considered the most glorious of my life. It was he who had given me the nickname "the Senegalese pilgrim," which my lack of modesty had led me to adopt without much protest. In 1759 he himself had made a short stopover in Senegal as part of a scientific voyage made under the direction of the renowned astronomer Nicolas-Louis de la Caille. The expedition, intended to enable scientists to observe the passage of Halley's comet in the sky above Madagascar, had been a failure: on the night of its passage, clouds had blocked the comet from view. But Le Joyand, who always made the best of everything, liked to tell stories of that voyage from his youth. He gloried in being something of a connoisseur of the beauty of Wolof women, despite the brevity of his stay in Senegal.

"Take a good look, Adanson. Don't you think she resembles the women that you and I both saw in Senegal?"

He told me her name was Madeleine and that she came from Guadeloupe. She was the servant of some friends of his from Angers, the Benoist-Cavays, who had bought her when she disembarked from a ship that had sailed to Guadeloupe from the island of Gorée. She had been only four years old at the time and remembered nothing of her homeland. But her face spoke for her. Le Joyand was certain that she belonged to the Wolof race.

"Don't you think, as I do, Adanson, that she looks Wolof?"

All his guests were admiring the portrait of Madeleine, and Le Joyand, the center of attention, did not give me time to respond. I would not have been capable of saying anything anyway, so tight was my throat.

His friends the Benoist-Cavays had a sister-in-law, Marie-Guillemine Benoist, a talented artist, who had decided to paint the portrait of their beautiful servant. When they had learned that Le Joyand wished to hang this portrait on a wall of his salon in honor of Michel Adanson, her owners had not hesitated to ask the artist to lend it to him. Marie-Guillemine Benoist had agreed to be separated from it for only two days.

"So would you confirm, Adanson, as I keep telling the Benoist-Cavays, that Madeleine really is a Black of Wolof origin, and not Bambara?"

I had enough presence of mind to reply to Le Joyand that yes, without doubt, the young woman in the portrait was of

Wolof origin, and that I had even known a young woman in Senegal who strangely resembled her. The same long neck, the same aquiline nose, the same mouth . . .

I did not have time to pronounce Maram's name. Already, Le Joyand, who was stubbornly determined to make me happy, was leading me, along with all his other guests, toward some chairs arranged in a semicircle around a few music stands. I was given a front-row seat, and no sooner had I sat down than I discovered that one of the women whom I had distractedly greeted in the entrance hall was an opera singer. She introduced herself to me very graciously and told me that she was going to sing—accompanied by a violin, a cello, an oboe, and a flute—extracts from the third act of Gluck's *Orpheus and Eurydice*.

This was no mere coincidence: I had been weak enough once to tell Le Joyand that the only opera I had seen in my life was that very work by Gluck. So he had arranged to have a few pieces played for me that day, as if trying to prove to me, while I was still alive, the strength of his friendship for me.

When the musicians performed the prelude to the singer's first songs, I had to recognize that I felt grateful to Le Joyand for having organized this concert, because it seemed to me that, during the time that the music was being played, I would be able to disentangle myself from my emotions. But I was wrong. I broke down when the singer, a soprano, began to voice Eurydice's lamentations because Orpheus, having descended to the underworld, did not dare look at her. Behind the musicians, I caught sight of Madeleine's portrait and, overcome by a sort of delirium of the imagination, had the feeling that Maram was borrowing the soprano's voice to reproach me for the oblivion

238 · DAVID DIOP

into which I had cast her. Maram seemed distant and close at the same time, present and absent from her own portrait. Her face wore the expression that I imagined Eurydice's must have worn when, happy at last to be looked at by Orpheus, she suddenly understood, in the very moment when death took her again, the meaning of her husband's feigned indifference. I had lived that brief instant, that time suspended between life and death, with Maram. I was her Orpheus; she was my Eurydice. But, unlike the Gluck opera, with its happy ending, I had lost Maram forever.

The flood of memories, which I had held back for decades behind a dam of illusions to save me from their cruelty, now submerged me. And I saw the singer's eyes glisten with tears at the sight of an old man losing his composure like that before her.

Despite all my efforts to block it out, the ordeal on the pier in Gorée, after our brief escape beyond the door to the voyage of no return, came back to me intact. I realized then that painting and music have the power to reveal to ourselves our secret humanity. Through art, we can sometimes push open a hidden door leading to the darkest part of our being, as black as the depths of a prison cell. And, once that door is wide open, the corners of our soul are so brightly illuminated that our lies to ourselves no longer have an inch of shade in which they can take refuge, as if exposed to the African sun at its zenith.

My dear Aglaé, I am now coming to the end of the story I wished to tell you, and to the end of my life. I dare to hope that when I finish writing my notebooks, you will discover them inside the red Morocco-leather portfolio, in the place where I will hide them for you. The uncertainty as to whether you will one day discover this secret part of my past inside a hidden drawer will torment me until death, which is, I feel, close. But it seems necessary to me to test your loyalty in that way. This test will, I believe, prove that you have understood all the invisible chains that have weighed down my existence.

If you accepted it as your legacy, you will also have found, in one of the drawers of the hibiscus cabinet, a necklace of white and blue glass beads which I brought back from Senegal. I beg you to go to Angers or to Paris, to visit the people whom Madeleine serves, and to give her this necklace on my behalf. Claude-François Le Joyand can provide you with their address. If he refuses, as I think possible, offer him one or two of my shell collections in exchange. He will be able to use those collections to land the position he covets at the Institute.

Unlike older Africans sent to the Americas, who often transport, in little leather sachets, a few seeds from plants of their own country, Madeleine was probably not able to take anything with her. She was too young when she was abducted from Senegal. And since neither my name nor my person will mean anything to her, I beg you to add to that modest necklace a louis d'or that you will find in the same drawer. Tell Madeleine that, if she wishes to, she may spend that gold coin celebrating the memory of a very young man who never truly returned from his voyage to Senegal. Madeleine looks so much like Maram! See her for me. Talk to her about me, or don't tell her anything. Go to see her and you will see me!

XXXVI

Madeleine hated her portrait. She did not recognize herself and she had the feeling that it would bring her bad luck for the rest of her life. The men who saw it stared at her afterward as if they wanted to undress her. The more boorish among them tried to touch her breasts. Even Monsieur Benoist, her master, took liberties. Madame, who was jealous by nature, had divined everything.

Ever since she had posed for the artist—Monsieur Beno-ist's sister-in-law—strange things had happened to her. It was as if the painting was speaking on her behalf, saying all sorts of nonsense to anyone who looked at it. Only the day before, a lady had come to offer her a cheap African necklace and a louis d'or so she could drink to the health of a dead man, a certain Michel Danson, or something like that. She had refused both gifts. She was not something to be bought or sold. Not anymore: she had, for all her remembered life, belonged to the Benoist-Cavays. They had emancipated her but she was not free.

The lady had been very insistent. It was not charity, she said. She was giving Madeleine the necklace and the louis d'or to respect the last wishes of her father, who had been to

Africa. Before dying, he had seen her portrait. She looked exactly like a certain Mara, or something like that. Mara was
a young Senegalese woman whom Michel Danson had loved
when he was young.

Madeleine had said no. She did not want another woman's
gifts. It was not her fault if Michel Danson had mixed her up
with someone else. The lady had wept as she went away, still
holding her treasures. Madeleine knew she had done the right
thing. In the past, she had made herself cry by torturing herself with impossible questions. She remembered nothing of
Senegal and did not want to remember anything. They had
taken her away from Africa but left her memory behind. She
had been too young. Sometimes, snatches of song and flashes
of sunlight reflected by the sea would come to her in dreams.
That was all.

Her home was not over there in Senegal; her home was
Capesterre-de-Guadeloupe. She hoped that the Benoist-
Cavays would soon decide to return to their property on the
island. Above all, she hoped that they would leave her portrait
in France and that nobody in Capesterre would see her hung
on a wall in her masters' house, her right breast bared.

At home, in Capesterre, she knew only one old man who
remembered everything. It was old Orpheus, who—on days
when he'd had too much rum to drink—would tell anyone
who'd listen that his name was Makou and that he came from
an African desert called Lapoule, or something like that. To
make fun of him, instead of calling him Orpheus, the name
that Monsieur Benoist's father had given him when he arrived at the plantation, they nicknamed him Makou Lapoule.
When he was drunk, he would always say that he had become

a slave after being cursed by a white demon when he was a very small child.

Makou was absolutely convinced that he and his sister had been kidnapped because he had pulled the hair of a white man who had appeared one day out of nowhere in his village in Africa, when he was still only a baby. Makou Lapoule swore that his older sister had had time to tell him the whole story before they were separated during the departure of the ship that took them to hell. He had been eight years old, she had been twelve. He had not forgotten anything. And whenever he was drunk he would repeat in his hoarse voice that he should never have clung to that white man's red hair when he was a baby, that this was why he had become a slave. Red hair was the mark of a demon.

The others made fun of him, they laughed at him, but I—Madeleine—did not laugh in the same way. I laughed to stop myself weeping over Orpheus's ravings.